IMPERSONATION

IMPERSONATION

THE GHOST SQUADRON BOOK 5

SARAH NOFFKE
MICHAEL ANDERLE

LMBPN

DISRUPTIVE IMAGINATION

IMPERSONATION TEAM

JIT Beta Readers -
From all of us, our deepest gratitude!

Larry Omans
Kelly O'Donnell
Paul Westman
Sarah Weir
Tim Adams
Micky Cocker
James Caplan
John Ashmore
Joshua Ahles
Peter Manis
Kimberly Boyer

*If we missed anyone, **please** let us know!*

Editor
Lynne Stiegler

For Lydia. My greatest treasure in the universe.
-Sarah

To Family, Friends and
Those Who Love
To Read.
May We All Enjoy Grace
To Live the Life We Are
Called.
- Michael

Dex's Parts and Manufacturing, Planet Kezza, Tangki System

Julianna was peeking through the spokes of the old Stutz Bearcat when the aliens arrived. She remained hidden as the six pirates sauntered into the mechanic's shop of the oversized warehouse. With teeth clenched, she glared at the intruders.

Fucking pirates might steal and destroy, but at least they were punctual, Julianna thought.

You know what I'm thinking right now? Pip asked in Julianna's head.

She rolled her eyes but smiled still. *That it's the perfect time to distract me?*

Oh, dear, Julianna. It's not always about you, you know. One of these days I'm going to get a life of my own, and then it will be about me.

Is there a reason you're bothering me right now? Julianna

squinted, watching the backs of the Kezzin pirates as they huddled around Dex, the owner of the business.

There are a few reasons, actually. The first is this car. I know someone who would like it. Julianna looked at the decrepit vehicle. *That's very thoughtful of you.*

I'm considered extremely thoughtful—ask anyone. But I realize you don't always notice because you have a lot on your mind, Pip said with a loud laugh. **Mind! Get it?**

Julianna shook her head, securing her pistol in her holster just as the largest pirate shoved Dex in the chest. The owner of the warehouse was a sizeable man with a round belly and thick arms, but he was no match for the alien.

Also, I've been thinking about going on a health kick. Thoughts? Pip continued.

I don't even know what to say about that. You're an AI.

With feelings!

Fine, fine. What does this health kick involve? Julianna asked, humoring him. Two of the pirates had picked up long pipes and were slapping them into their palms. It was almost showtime.

Well, a cleanse would be necessary. I've been considering going vegan. What do you think?

I don't have the first clue how that would work. You don't eat, Pip.

It's mostly just food for thought.

Oh, no you didn't...

In fact, I did. But maybe *you* should consider going vegan.

Let's discuss this later. Right now I'm busy.

Dex shook his head furiously and yelled, "I don't have what you want!" at the pirate. The Kezzin grabbed Dex's shirt and lifted him into the air.

"If you don't have our money, we'll take the parts," the pirate bellowed. He turned his ugly lizard face to the brutes beside him. "Load up everything we can carry. We'll sell it."

Julianna slid soundlessly around the Stutz Bearcat, still mostly out of view. The pirates were too busy creating havoc to notice her standing roughly ten feet off the ground on the wide shelf.

The Kezzin holding Dex in the air laughed. "We were going to take parts anyway *and* the money."

"I'm going to need you to lower Dex," Julianna yelled from the shelf.

All the Kezzin froze and the lead pirate turned, his narrow eyes enlarging. "Well, hey there, sweetheart. You want me to pick *you* up? I can do that." He looked at the closest pirate. "Let's take her too."

With a hungry look on his face, the Kezzin ambled forward, dropping the pipe he'd had in his hands. *That was a big mistake.*

"Come here, little human," a Kezzin sneered.

"You want me to come over there? Okay." Julianna backed up a step, careful not to bump the car, then ran forward and leapt. The Kezzin hadn't expected the attack, so like a coward, he covered his head with his arms.

The heel of Julianna's boot smashed into his torso and he slammed to the ground. The pirate holding Dex shoved the mechanic forward and spun to Julianna.

"Get her," he ordered in a low and dangerous voice. His lackeys spread out with leering grins.

Stupid woman was about to get hers.

Julianna scooped the pipe from the floor, hefted it to feel the balance, then spun on the balls of her feet to drive it into the nearest Kezzin face.

He gurgled through his broken face, before gagging and gasping on his way to the floor.

Julianna darted away. Two pirates followed. An old airplane stood in the middle of the warehouse floor. She ran for it, slowing to let the pirates get close. When she reached the propeller, she grabbed it, spun around and slammed two feet into the chest of the closest Kezzin. He bounced off the other and the two went down.

Julianna was on them in a flash, cracking their heads together as she looked for more enemies. It wouldn't do to have them sneaking up behind her.

"Get her, already you sons of whores!" the lead pirate screamed.

Two others approached, more warily. She took off at an angle and they followed. She disappeared behind a crate and they spread out, one taking each side. She jumped up, landing lightly on the top. The Kezzin both saw the movement. They reached up, but were too slow.

She kicked the nearest in the face and did a back flip over the other. He almost fell over as he tried to follow her movements. She body-blocked him into the crate, seized him by his collar and the seat of his pants, lifting him and swinging him like a battering ram. With his head jammed through the wood, she dropped his body.

Only one left -- the so-called leader. Julianna slowly

removed her pistol from the holster and took aim. He froze where he was.

"Trying to sneak around behind me while your boys were a diversion? That's not very manly." Julianna waved her pistol toward the entrance. "Take this scum and get the fuck out of here. If I find out you've bothered Dex again, I'm going to tear off your balls and shove them down your throat."

Julianna's aim held steady, her eyes intense.

"Do I make myself clear?"

"Y-y-yeah," the pirate stuttered, stumbling backwards.

Julianna waited until she was sure they were gone before putting her pistol back in its holster. Damn it, Ghost Squadron needed to get better weapons. And soon.

For now the weapons were fine, since she was mostly fighting poor pirates who used their fists because they didn't have anything else. Reduced trade of weapons was the handiwork of Ghost Squadron. They'd been cleaning up illegal dealers, but for every one they shut down two more opened. That was why there was no time to sleep— not that rest was entirely necessary.

Julianna looked around, impressed that she hadn't made as big a mess as she'd expected.

Dex, however, had had his shirt ripped and earned a bash to the head from the pirates. Still, he was mostly unharmed. He scanned the warehouse while catching his breath.

"Is it just you?" he asked, perhaps expecting more people to jump out from behind the shelves.

"Yeah. You said roughly six pirates bullied you." Julianna stretched her neck from side to side, loosening up after the fight. She hadn't broken a sweat, but the adrenaline rush had been nice.

"Oh… Well, I expected… When we talked, you said that your team would help with the pirates," Dex said, confusion making his forehead wrinkle.

"The team is busy." Julianna swept her arm at the warehouse filled with parts. "We still have a deal, right? I got rid of your pirate problem, so you'll load my ship with supplies?"

Dex nodded. "Yeah. I'm a man of my word. I've got you covered. However, I've got a question. I saw the list of things you need, and it's quite a lot."

"Those pirates were going to take a whole bunch more than I'm asking for," Julianna said.

"No, no, it's not that," Dex began. "It's just that based on all you asked for…well, you must be outfitting a massive ship."

Julianna smiled to herself, a new pride in her chest at the thought of *Ricky Bobby*. "Oh, yeah. It's impressive. A battlecruiser."

"It must be, to need all the parts you've requested," Dex said, awe written on his face. "Just one more question, and you don't have to answer if you don't want to."

"Go on, then," Julianna said. She liked the old mechanic. He was a good man—one who had been bullied on Kezza, which he'd tried to make his home.

"Who does this battlecruiser belong to?" Dex asked.

Julianna smiled widely. "Me. It's my ship."

Landing Bay, *Ricky Bobby*, Tangki System

Although technically *Ricky Bobby* was both her and
Eddie's ship, for simplicity's sake Julianna had been brief
with Dex. She never tired of saying it..."her ship." She
popped out of the Q-Ship after landing on *Ricky Bobby*,
motioning to the closest crew member.

"Parts need to go to Dr. A'Din Hatcherik's lab," she said,
striding around a construction area. The whole ship was in
renovation mode, which was why Eddie hadn't accompa-
nied Julianna.

"Tell me it wasn't any fun," Eddie said to her. He was
standing on the top step of a ladder holding a beam up
with one hand, although it was incredibly heavy. Knox
stood on a neighboring scaffold with a fistful of wires, and
his brow was scrunched as he worked on the repair.

"It was so fucking boring." Julianna pretended to yawn.
"The pirates didn't even put up a serious fight. It was over
before I knew it."

Lars set the transport ship down with ease, and a sort of smile could be seen on his face through the windshield. The Kezzin had obviously enjoyed returning to his home planet, a place he'd never thought he'd see again. And seeing his brother's face when he'd landed the transport ship had been priceless, even for Julianna. Sharing someone else's pride-filled moment was almost as good as having one herself.

"Did you get everything I asked for?" Hatch asked, waddling out from behind the cargo boxes that had already been unloaded.

"Not only did I get everything on your Christmas List," Julianna began, "I also got you a surprise."

"Surprise?" the Londil queried with skepticism on his octopus face.

"Check it out for yourself." Julianna motioned to the lowered ramp at the back of the transport ship.

Hatch rolled his eyes but hurried over, curiosity obvious in his expression. He paused in front of the open door, his mouth popping open. "Is that…"

Julianna crossed her arms and nodded proudly. "It is."

"How did you get this?" Hatch asked.

"It was actually Pip's idea," Julianna confessed.

Giving me credit…that was nice of you. I'm not interfaced with the ship yet, chirped Pip in Julianna's head.

Which means you couldn't have told on me if I had taken credit.

You're a real pal, Julianna.

"Tell Pip that I owe him. I'll have him interfaced with the ship soon to show my gratitude," Hatch said.

"I'm not sure that should take priority over upgrading the gate drives," Ricky Bobby said from the speakers. "They aren't up to Federation standards, and if we need to make a quick exit that will pose a problem."

Julianna smiled inwardly. AI rivalry. She'd suspected this would happen. Ricky Bobby had transitioned to *Unsurpassed* without issue, and having her old AI in charge of their new ship felt incredibly right. However, there were still things that would take time, and convincing the two AIs to cooperate was one of them.

"What is it? What did the Commander bring you?" Knox asked, hurrying over after climbing quickly down. The guy wasn't afraid of heights, and was as coordinated up high as a monkey in a tree.

"It's...it's something I've only seen pictures of," Hatch said as a crew member pushed the Stutz Bearcat down the ramp and onto the deck.

"Whoa!" Knox exclaimed. "That's incredible."

Eddie strode over and halted beside Julianna. "How did you score a Stutz Bearcat?"

"I asked," she answered frankly. "I simply asked."

"*Damn* that Fregin charm. If you ever use it on me I'll be in trouble," Eddie said.

Julianna shook her head. "Captain, I think you're confusing a simple request with some sort of magic."

Eddie smiled broadly. "Oh, that's cute. You don't see it."

"See what?" Julianna asked.

"Your knack for persuasion," Eddie said, winking at her.

"Again, I simply asked, 'Can you include the car?' That's how it happened," Julianna explained.

Eddie shook his head and whistled. "Damn, that mechanic never stood a chance."

"Teach, you've been inhaling paint fumes for too long," Julianna said, and strode over to Hatch. He was already flattened under the old car.

"Julie, this is incredible. I never expected to own a gem like this," Hatch said, his voice vibrating with excitement.

"We're glad you like it. Think you'll be able to restore the car?" Julianna asked.

"The engine needs to be rebuilt," Hatch said, sliding out from underneath the Bearcat.

"And the hoses all need to be replaced," Knox added from under the hood.

Hatch slapped two tentacles together jovially. "But yes. We can have this baby up and running in no time."

A cough echoed from overhead.

"Yes, of course. Ricky Bobby is right," Julianna said, taking the mild hint from the AI. "We need to get the gate drives online first."

"And the cloaks," Eddie added.

"Yeah, yeah. You'll get your ship upgraded," Hatch grumbled as he waddled off. "Can't even take a day off for my hobbies."

Knox ran after him, almost bouncing. "Think how good that car is going to look next to your Bugatti and the Volkswagen bug."

"Only a few more, and my collection will be complete," Hatch said to the young mechanic as they sped off. "A '57 Corvette, a 1970 Plymouth 'Cuda, a DeLorean…" His voice faded as they walked out of the bay.

Eddie turned to Julianna. "Think we'll need a bigger ship to house Hatch's car collection."

I found interesting information on the VW bug, Pip interjected in Julianna's head.

Like the fact that it was commissioned originally by Adolf Hitler?

Like the fact that making out in the backseat is considered extremely uncomfortable.

How... What? We really need to restrict the things you can search for.

Speaking of searching, I've been doing more enquiry on this vegan business.

"Oh dear," Julianna said aloud.

Eddie gave her a curious glance. "Pip?" he asked, having read it on her face.

She nodded.

If I was in the captain's head I could easily share the information I found on vegan recipes. Did you know there's a cashew cheese that's very smooth?

No. And no. There's no way I'm giving up meat or cheese.

This is about living your best life, Julianna.

I'm starting to consider that involves ending you.

"Julianna and Eddie," Ricky Bobby called. "Jack requests your presence in his office."

Julianna sighed, laughing to herself. She could never guess what crazy thing Pip would come up with next.

"Tell him we'll be right there," Eddie said, laughing too.

Although he wasn't privy to the jokes, he still seemed to enjoy the entertainment Julianna got from Pip. Maybe she *should* consider allowing him in both their heads. She just wasn't sure how that would change things.

3

Jack Renfro's Office, *Ricky Bobby*, Tangki System

A drumming sound filled Jack's office. Julianna and Eddie entered to find the spymaster for the Federation tapping his hands on the surface of his desk and looking around the office like he'd lost something. He clicked his tongue absentmindedly, not noticing the two standing squarely in front of him.

"You rang?" Eddie chirped.

Jack raised his chin and blinked at them. "Yes. Right." He scattered a stack of papers, looking through them for something specific.

"ArchAngel kept telling you that you needed better organization," Julianna teased.

At the mention of the AI, Jack's eyes widened. "She liked to tell me a lot of things."

"Does it bother you, boss, that your new office belonged to a crazy mastermind?" Eddie asked, strolling the length of the long office. It was much nicer than the one he'd had before, since Felix had invested heavily in putting the nicest furniture into his personal space.

"I got over it rather quickly, especially since my chair has a massage mode." Jack nestled into the leather seat, but his look of comfort slipped away after a moment.

"You still miss ArchAngel, don't you?" Julianna observed that there was something different about Jack. His dark hair, which was usually slicked back smoothly, looked a bit chaotic, as if he'd run his fingers through it. His button-up shirt was creased, and its sleeves had been rolled up.

Jack straightened. "ArchAngel? Oh, no. I mean, we have Ricky Bobby now and General Reynolds has his ship back. That's all that matters."

He misses her, Pip teased in Julianna's head.

They spent a lot of time together.

We spend a lot of time together.

So...

So maybe you should miss me when I'm away or go quiet.

When exactly is that? How about we play the quiet game and you give me a chance to miss you? Make yourself scarce.

Fine, but you *will* miss me. Wait and see.

I'm waiting...

"Oh, here it is." Jack pulled a report from a stack. "Intel came from General Reynolds recently. It's a very curious case."

"You have our attention," Eddie said. He slid out one of the chairs in front of Jack's new desk and offered it to Julianna, but she shook her head. She didn't really like to sit unless she was flying. Eddie took the seat, pressing his elbows onto his knees as he leaned forward.

"There was a theft inside Jaslene Corporation," Jack began, scanning the report.

"Why do I know that name?" Julianna asked.

Jack nodded. "We contracted with them to build secure storage units. They're known for their high-tech impenetrable units."

"That's right," Julianna said.

"Is it ironic that they had a theft when they're known for their security?" Eddie asked.

"You'd think so, but the person who stole valuable records was the CEO of the corporation, Mary Jaslene," Jack told them.

Eddie scratched his head. "Maybe I'm a bit thick, but how can a CEO steal records from her own corporation?"

Jack set down the report and stood, as if adrenaline had suddenly infected him. "Because we believe the real Mary Jaslene's testimony, and she states that she was on vacation on the day of the theft. According to her, she didn't come into the office. However, the security cameras clearly show that someone who looked exactly like the CEO entered the building."

"Okay, that's bizarre," Eddie said.

"What did this imposter take?" Julianna asked.

Jack held up a finger as he paced. "Good question. This person removed records that only Mary Jaslene had access to. You see, when the Federation contracted her company to build the secure storage units, we requested that the information not be disseminated companywide. The contents of those units is classified, so we didn't want our enemies to discover their locations."

"That's what was stolen, wasn't it?" Julianna guessed.

"Bingo." Jack halted, turning toward them. "There are two Federation storage facilities located on the frontier, and whoever impersonated Mary Jaslene now knows where they are."

"What's stored in these units?" Eddie asked.

"*That* I'm working on finding out, but I'm pretty sure there's already someone on our staff who knows the answer because he created the technology," Jack said.

Eddie looked up at Julianna, who was still stoically standing. "Hatch!"

"Jack, you said Jaslene Corporation is known for their high levels of security. Even if these guys have the locations, should we really be worried that they can break into them and get whatever they're after?" Julianna argued.

"I'm fairly certain that we should be *very* concerned," Jack said. "From what I could figure out, the alien species that pulled off the theft shouldn't be underestimated. If they could break into Jaslene Corporation, they can probably find a way to rob a storage unit."

"Oh, goody. Have you figured out what alien species we're dealing with?" Eddie asked, eagerly rubbing his hands together.

"Marilla will have more information on them. There's not much known on the Saverus, but I'm certain she can shine some light," Jack said.

"Did you say 'the Saverus?'" Julianna asked. "I didn't think they actually existed."

Jack nodded. "I've heard of them too, but only briefly. It appears that this race of shapeshifters is indeed real, and potentially highly dangerous."

4

Intelligence Center, *Ricky Bobby*, Tangki System

"I think that we should put the hoop right over your desk," Chester said, aiming the foam basketball with one eye shut before launching it at an invisible hoop. It banged into the wall behind Marilla's desk before landing on her keyboard.

She looked up, pretending to be annoyed. "I think—"

"Oh, shush," Chester said, spinning to his main workstation. "This is my new favorite song." He turned up the volume.

"It's a hundred years old or more!" Marilla said.

"Tsk, tsk. Taylor Swift is timeless, and you damn well know it." Chester picked up another foam ball from his desk and spun back, aiming it threateningly at Marilla. The new Intelligence Center was even better than the last. Marilla's workstation was larger, and positioned right behind Chester's—and surprisingly, once they had loaded up the space with all the workstations he needed, there was absolutely no room for anyone else. Just Chester and Mar. Oh, well and Harley, of course.

The shaggy dog peeked up from the floor, the orange ball having caught his eye. Chester faked a throw at Marilla, then tossed the ball toward the door and Harley charged after it, tail wagging.

Harley darted into the hallway, catching the foam ball in his mouth as he slid into the wall.

"Good catch," Eddie told him as he and Julianna approached.

The dog looked up and bounded in their direction. Tail wagging, he dutifully brought the ball over to Julianna. She paid him no attention and continued moving forward, making him walk backward to keep his brown eyes on her.

"He brought you a present," Eddie said, pointing to the ball.

Unhurriedly Julianna peered down at the dog, looking unimpressed. "I prefer whiskey and chocolate."

"He remembers that you saved his life. I don't think you're going to be able to stop his obsession now," Eddie teased.

"He licks his own butt. I think it's very likely that he'll forget," Julianna said, rounding into the Intelligence Center.

"Or are you hoping that *you'll* forget?" Eddie prodded. "Jules cared enough to save Harley. She must like him, despite the tough-girl act."

Julianna looked down at Harley, now giving him a

meaningful expression. "No good deed goes unpunished, am I right?"

Harley hopped as he barked, and the foam ball fell from his mouth and rolled under a workstation.

Chester nodded his head to the blaring music, dancing in his seat and singing loudly.

"Nice singing," Eddie said. He shot Marilla a wide smile, jerking a thumb in Chester's direction. "That's real entertainment."

"It's nonstop entertainment, is what it is," Marilla replied.

As the music faded, Eddie stared around the new Intelligence Center. It had remarkably made significant progress in a short time. There appeared to be enough computer power to hack the Federation if they so desired. What there wasn't, were chairs—only Chester's and Marilla's.

"I understand you can offer us insights on the Saverus species," Julianna said, her attention on Marilla although Harley kept pawing at her knee.

"Yes. I reviewed the information Jack sent over, and I can confirm that they are the most likely candidates for this imposter job," Marilla said.

"Why are you so sure?" Julianna asked.

"When Ms. Jaslene's office was searched after the theft was discovered, the team found scales in the carpet," Marilla explained.

"Scales? Like measuring devices?" Eddie asked.

Marilla shook her head, typing on her computer and taking over the largest monitor on the main wall. An image of a giant red snake with green eyes popped onto the screen. The alien's face had a strange, almost human quality about it—something in the eyes and the shape.

"Meet the Saverus," began Marilla. "In their original form they look like large snakes. They can grow arms for certain purposes, but as you can see here they are mostly a head, body, and tail."

"You're telling us that this snake can shift into the form of a human?" Eddie asked, giving Julianna a look of disbelief. She appeared to be in deep thought, or a rather in-depth conversation with Pip.

"Not just human. Saverus can become Kezzin, Trid, Londil, or any other species. They can hold up to six different personas at once," Marilla explained.

"And how do they steal these personas?" Julianna asked.

Marilla pushed her long braid off her shoulder. "They need only come in contact once with the person they wish to impersonate."

"So you're telling me that this giant snake visited Mary Jaslene? Wouldn't she have remembered that?" Eddie asked.

"Maybe, but probably not," Marilla said. "I'd guessed that it took on a different form—a more acceptable one—when it came in contact with Ms. Jaslene."

"I thought this species was a myth," Julianna said, eyeing the image skeptically.

"It's true that we know little of the Saverus, but they did in fact exist." Marilla rose from her computer station and walked around it. "They came from the planet Savern, but oddly there are none there anymore. A Saverus sighting is rare and it was thought that they'd become extinct."

"Or were hiding while disguised," Julianna said, her tone careful.

Marilla nodded. "That's my thought too. What I've been able to find out about their society is quite strange. They had a weird hierarchical system that was ritually-oriented."

"How so?" Eddie prodded.

"Well, the lower ranks appear to answer to the elders. And they are only placed into a role once they pass a series of sacramental tests," Marilla explained, twisting a rogue strand of hair around her finger. "What I know is incomplete, since there's little information on them. It's strange. When I went to research the species...I don't know..."

"What?" Julianna encouraged.

"I don't know. It's almost like the records have been erased." Marilla, who had looked lost in thought, gazed up at them. "Is it possible that they've intentionally been trying to hide?"

"It's absolutely possible, because the best way to pull off a major heist is for no one to know you exist," Julianna stated.

"Is there anything else you can tell us about this mysterious alien species?" Eddie asked.

"Tell them about the rat people," Chester said, his tone dripping with excitement.

"Rat people? Oh no, who are they?" Julianna asked.

"The Petigrens," Marilla stated. "And they are—or they were—the Saverus' servants."

Eddie was about to ask another question, but he was knocked off-balance when something rocked into the ship, making all four of them lurch forward from the assault.

5

Bridge, *Ricky Bobby*, Tangki System

"What the fuck?" Eddie blurted when the ship was rocked by a second attack.

"Ricky Bobby," Julianna called as they entered the bridge, Harley on their heels. "What's going on?"

Fletcher was there as usual and was scanning the central radar, his brow furrowed. He pointed to a series of red dots on the starboard side of the battlecruiser.

"I've intercepted the enemy's communications," Ricky Bobby said from overhead. "It appears these Trids think Felix is aboard. I'm holding them off the best the ship can manage in its current state."

The battlecruiser bucked as more missiles impacted the hull.

Eddie grunted with frustration. "Well, it did used to belong to Felix."

"I thought Felix was friendly with the Trids," Fletcher said, rubbing his hand over his bald head. He was both young and old in Eddie's eyes. He had the spirit of a young man, but the wisdom and features of someone much older.

"I've examined many of Felix's records. They suggest that he was engaged in shady practices," Ricky Bobby informed them.

"Shocking," Julianna muttered.

"So he employed the Trids and then screwed them. Yeah, no surprise there," Eddie said.

"Sleep with a dog and you're going to get fleas," Fletcher said.

Harley, who was standing at Julianna's feet, barked at this, seemingly offended.

Eddie cast the dog a furtive glance. *That dog might be smarter than they all realize,* he thought. No wonder he preferred Julianna to anyone else.

"The enemy's ships are closing. Without the cloaks and with the gate drives offline we're going to need a more direct defense," Ricky Bobby informed them.

Eddie imagined that from the engine room he could hear Hatch yelling, "I know! I'm working on it, damn it!"

Julianna turned to Eddie. "The Black Eagles. They'll be the best defense against the Stingrays."

"*We* have a Stingray, remember?" Eddie began. "I could take that fish out and get in close. Blow them up without them seeing me coming."

"That's a good plan, but there are too many." She pointed to the radar table. Two dozen Stingrays were approaching slowly, maneuvering around Ricky Bobby's counterattacks. "When they figure out it's you attacking them, you'll be outnumbered. My instincts say to leave our Stingray behind for another time."

Eddie nodded. He trusted Julianna's instinct like it was a life line. "Okay, then we're off." He ran for the landing bay.

"Stay on the comm," Julianna called to his back.

"You said you've intercepted their comms, right?" Julianna asked Ricky Bobby.

"That's correct," he answered.

"Then will you inform them that we don't have Felix Castile and are not their enemy?" Julianna knew it was a long shot, but although she craved a good fight she didn't like to kill unnecessarily. It felt wasteful, even the Trids.

"I tried that," Ricky Bobby informed her, his tone morose.

"And they didn't believe you, because that's exactly what the real Felix would have said...is that right?" Fletcher asked from Julianna's side.

Harley kept growling softly at the Lieutenant. Aboard *Ricky Bobby* Fletcher had taken a hands-on approach, helping with crew assignments and workflow. Jack may have been right that he would make a good choice for XO. This battle might be the time to tell them.

Fletcher had combat experience and was a respected leader, but the hardest thing for soldiers to do in battle was exactly what he and Julianna were doing—manage the battle from a strategic level, leaving the tactics to those engaged on the front lines. She would have loved to fly into battle alongside Eddie, but there were too many unknowns with the new ship and having a bird's-eye view was crucial for a battle of this magnitude.

The battlecruiser jerked violently under a fresh barrage. Alarms echoed throughout the ship.

"Ricky Bobby, status?" Julianna called, gripping the radar table for support.

"A flight of Stingrays snuck through our defenses on the starboard side. The missiles are keeping them back, but not targeting them well enough for complete protection," Ricky Bobby said.

"Damn it, can we get some railguns already?" Julianna said, gritting her teeth.

"I might know a guy," Fletcher said with a wink.

"Make sure we survive this battle so you can call your contact in time for the next. I'm tired of eating bullets because we're the Federation's secret squadron." Julianna paced back and forth in front of the radar table, watching as the Black Eagles deployed from *Ricky Bobby*. "Come on, Eddie—get those fuckers off our tail."

The Black Eagles streaked into the void of space with Eddie in the lead. It felt good to be back in the pilot's seat, cruising in the direction of a bunch of Stingrays. Most could appreciate the adrenaline rush, but for Eddie it was more. Each battle he fought was an attempt to come back to himself. Trying to make amends for what he'd done—or really, what he hadn't done.

"Carnivore, I'd like to make this fish fry happen as fast and efficient as possible," Eddie said over the comm.

"Copy that, Blackbeard," Lars responded.

Behind the Kezzin pilot were three other Black Eagles. Lone Wolf, Escrema, and Trapeze were their best pilots, and at the moment the only ones prepared for this level of combat. Recruitment efforts had taken a backseat to renovations.

"Lone Wolf and Escrema, take the Stingrays that have broken through defenses on starboard," Eddie ordered.

"Yes, sir," the pilots said in unison.

"Trapeze, you come with us. Let's go after that school of fish ahead," Eddie said, speeding in the direction of a dozen Stingrays flying in formation.

Eddie pulled in a long, steadying breath and fired a barrage of bullets at the enemy ships. He swerved between two Stingrays trying to box him in, banking hard and whipping the ship around.

"Fuck yeah, baby! Feels good to be back in action," he roared. He sped after the two Stingrays, intent on teaching them a lesson.

***

"They're outnumbered," Fletcher observed, leaning over the radar table.

Julianna balled her fists, squeezing tightly. "That shouldn't be a problem. Our ships are faster and better equipped."

"Yes, but the Stingrays have enhanced maneuverability, according to what I discovered in both Felix's records and Dr. Hatcherik's notes on the ships," Ricky Bobby stated.

"Keep searching. Maybe there's something else we can use."

"Damn, these fuckers just keep coming." Eddie said over the comm, breathing deeply. "What did Felix do to piss them off so badly?"

"Blackbeard," Julianna began. "You have three Stingrays on your tail. I hope you have a strategy for faking them out." She watched as the radar model of the Black Eagle swung one way and then the other, narrowly avoiding enemy fire.

"I'd like to say I have a brilliant plan, but I'm running out of ideas," Eddie said as three more Stingrays dropped on him.

"Damn it! I'm going in there," Julianna said, but stayed frozen. "Pip can fly another Q-Ship." She knew she should stay here to command, but it was growing increasingly difficult. *Follow your instincts,* she told herself.

"Or we pull out altogether and risk gating," Fletcher offered.

It wasn't a bad solution, except that Julianna hated to run. It meant that you kept running until caught. She preferred to conquer her enemy or send *them* fleeing. "There's got to be a way to make them tuck tail," she mused.

Harley barked loudly, making Julianna start. She chanced a glance at the dog.

"Seriously, you chase your own tail but suddenly you understand English?" she said to the dog, and he whimpered slightly.

"Lone Wolf here. We cleared most of the Stingrays from

starboard. Escrema is staying back, but I think I can offer relief," the pilot said over the comm.

"Get in there, Lone Wolf. We don't have much more time," Julianna ordered over the comm.

"The shields on *Ricky Bobby* appear to be holding, so even if the Stingrays continue their assaults on that side we should be okay," Fletcher offered.

"Good point. The best part of this inherited ship is the shields," Julianna commented. She remembered the first time that she'd encountered one of Felix's smaller transport ships that had these shields. Its attacks had been relentless, and yet had no effect. Currently though, with the overhaul in place, *Ricky Bobby* was in a vulnerable state and the shields weren't at a hundred percent.

"Escrema, abandon starboard attack and aid the others," Julianna ordered. They could take a few hits, but the Black Eagles were overwhelmed.

"I think I've found something," Ricky Bobby announced.

"What is it?" Julianna asked urgently.

"It appears that Felix was prepared for an attack of just this sort," Ricky Bobby explained. "He apparently knew the Trids were close to waging war on him, and his scientists developed a weapon specific to the Stingrays."

Julianna scanned the radar, her frustration mounting at the sheer number of Stingrays that kept appearing.

"You see, Stingray technology is based on—"

"Science lesson later, Ricky Bobby. We need the solution pronto," Julianna urged.

"It appears to be untested, but Felix had developed an

antielectrogravitic pulse," Ricky Bobby said. "If my findings are correct, the weapon has one good shot in it, which will freeze the engines of every single Stingray in the vicinity."

"So they'd stop flying?" Julianna said, hope suddenly springing to her chest.

"Yes. They would be immobilized for approximately thirty seconds," Ricky Bobby said.

"And our own ships?" Julianna asked.

"They'll be unaffected. Their engines run on a different technology," Ricky Bobby informed her.

"Good decision, leaving the Stingray docked," Fletcher said, giving her a proud smile.

Julianna nodded. Although they didn't know if this plan was solid—she had hope. "You said it was untested?"

"Yes. According to what I could find, Felix's ship hadn't had an opportunity to test it, since that would have involved having many Stingrays in close proximity," Ricky Bobby stated.

"And they used to be allies before Felix somehow screwed them," Julianna said, pressing the button to open the comm. "Blackbeard, we might have a solution for you. We're sending out a pulse that should immobilize the Stingrays."

"Fuck yeah! That's the best news all day," Eddie said through a ragged breath. He'd taken a few hits from what Julianna had seen, but his engines appeared to be nominal.

"You and your Eagles will have thirty seconds to get in there and get out. Got it?" Julianna asked.

"Copy that, Commander," Eddie said, his voice lightening.

"Ricky Bobby, send out the pulse on my command," Julianna said.

"Yes, Jules," Ricky Bobby agreed.

"Pilots, I think it would be best to feign a retreat," Julianna said over the comm. "Make them think they've won so they'll be more relaxed when we turn the tables. And their guns will still work, so you'll have to use stealth to your advantage."

"Copy that, Strong Arm," Eddie confirmed.

Julianna and Fletcher watched on the radar as the Black Eagles headed back toward the ship. The Stingrays hesitated momentarily.

"Ricky Bobby, send out pulse in three, two, and one," Julianna ordered.

"Antielectrogravitic pulse sent," Ricky Bobby said.

Julianna held her breath, anxiously watching the radar. The Black Eagles continued their retreat and the Stingrays hovered in place—and then began to fall out of formation one by one, the way a ship does when experiencing engine failure.

"The pulse was successful," Julianna said over the comm. "Get in there and do some damage. I want you all out of there in twenty seconds." That would give the Black Eagles sufficient time to return to the landing bay, offering them the protection they needed after a battle like this. Space combat was unique, in that it couldn't go on for too long before casualties were inevitable. There were too many dangerous variables.

"Ricky Bobby, send a message to our friends the Trids," Julianna said. "Tell them that this ship is no longer the *Unsurpassed*, and Felix Castile is dead. They can continue to attack and make enemies of us, but we have not asked for a war."

"Who shall I say the message is from?" Ricky Bobby asked.

"Tell them it's from Ghost Squadron," Julianna stated with pride. She watched the radar as the Black Eagles returned and the Stingrays that hadn't been demolished rose into formation, their engines back online. The Trids they'd left alive retreated. Julianna hadn't wanted to strike such a hard blow to her enemy's enemy, but they'd left her no choice.

6

Hatch's Lab, *Ricky Bobby*, Tangki System
Eddie admired the 1976 Cadillac Fleetwood Sixty
Special Talisman as they entered Hatch's new lab area. It
was more of a dedicated space than the cargo bay he'd
worked in on *ArchAngel*, and currently it was filled with
rows of classic cars which seemed to overwhelm the space.
Eddie leaned down and stared through the window at
the impressive interior of the car. He'd never seen so much
crushed velvet and polished wood inside a vehicle.
"Can we redo the interior of my Q-Ship to match this?"
Eddie asked.
"That's the most sensible request you've made of me in
a long time," Hatch called from the lab table where he was
fiddling with a device that looked like high-tech goggles.
"My question is," Julianna began, looking around at the
large yet cramped space, "how are you able to work on ship
upgrades with all these vehicles in here?"
"Julie, you know I like you. Don't make me change my

mind about that," Hatch said, no real annoyance in his voice.

"Meanwhile, I look at Hatch the wrong way and he writes me off for eternity," Eddie said with a laugh.

"That's because you're an idiot," Hatch replied, holding up the goggles and peering through them. They magnified his face, making his bulging eyes look even bigger. "And to answer your question, I think I'm working just fine, and it's probably *because* I have the company of my cars. They've been spread out in different places throughout the galaxy, but when we moved onto *Ricky Bobby* I figured they should all come together."

"Does that mean you've found your forever home?" Eddie teased. Knox secretly shot him a sideways grin and nodded from behind Hatch's back.

"I saw that, Gunner," Hatch chided at once, lowering the goggles.

Knox's eyes widened in sudden shock.

"Damn, do you have eyes in the back of your head?" Eddie asked, impressed.

"No, but those goggles have mirror technology," Pip said from overhead.

"Pip, what are you doing in here?" Julianna asked, looking confused.

"Oh, hi, Jules. It's been a while, hasn't it?" Pip said, sounding like he was taunting her. "Hatch missed me, so he interfaced me with his lab."

"What? Oh…" Julianna covered her forehead with her hand.

"Yes, he *missed* me. It felt good to be mi—"

Julianna cut Pip off. "Would you shut it?"

"See? She's always trying to silence me," Pip complained.

Hatch waddled over carrying the goggles. "It didn't take long to connect Pip to my lab. I assure you it didn't detract from any of my other projects."

"It's totally fine." Eddie offered the mechanic a sympathetic smile. "Actually, Jules and I have been talking and we do think that your workload—even for you—is too much. We'd like your focus to remain on the really special projects."

"Which means?" The pointed stare Hatch gave him wasn't the look of relief Eddie had expected.

"We were thinking of hiring a Chief Engineer," Eddie said. "Someone to oversee the ship's maintenance."

All of Hatch's tentacles launched into the air and began flapping around wildly. "Because you think that I can't handle ship repairs and—"

Julianna waved her arms in front of Hatch, trying to calm him. "That's not it at all. It's just that *Ricky Bobby* needs a lot of work, and it would monopolize your time when you're already trying to manage the crew and build new ships. We're asking too much of you."

Hatch immediately softened, his cheeks puffing out. "It *is* a lot, and both the ship and special projects should be a priority." He held up the goggles as if in validation of his point.

"Let's just think on it. If it's something you want, then Jack has some applicants. You can help advise us," Eddie stated.

This didn't endear him to Hatch at all, only earned him a contemptuous glare.

"Hatch is going to build me a body," Pip said.

"He's what?" Julianna asked, shocked.

"Not right now," Hatch said at once, looking embarrassed. "It was just an idea we had. Something for the future—a droid of sorts. Something he has control over."

"Or what about the idea of giving him super-control over his host's body?" Knox blurted out.

The three turned to the young mechanic at once. He dropped the tool in his hand, and a look of shame sprang to his face. "Sorry. It was just a random idea I had. Really stupid. I won't interrupt again."

"More like brilliant…or rather satisfactory," Hatch said, correcting himself.

Knox's normally pale face flushed pink.

"What do you think?" Hatch asked, looking at Julianna. "What if Pip had control over your body? He might be able to enhance your movements during battle, taking into account specific factors for jumping, running, et cetera. It would be purely for emergency purposes. A failsafe, if you would."

Julianna didn't hesitate. "Hell no."

"If you were incapacitated in an emergency, then—"

"There's no way I'm giving him control," Julianna cut Hatch off. "He'll have me eating rice cakes and vegan hotdogs."

"They're delicious, Julianna," Pip teased.

"How would you know?" she spat at her AI.

"I don't, but I would if you'd let me take control. Think of it as 'autopilot mode.' That way you can go to sleep, and I can keep us working," Pip said.

Adamantly she shook her head. "No. I'll wake up

wearing makeup and high heels."

"I've always wanted to know how you'd look in something fancy," Pip mused.

"Get your own body," she shot back.

"*I'd* do it," Eddie said quickly. Hatch and Julianna stared at him with different levels of disbelief on their faces. Julianna's expression was more of a look of horror.

"Ding! Ding! Ding!" Pip yelled. "We have a winner."

"Eddie, are you sure?" Hatch asked, but before he could answer Julianna interrupted.

"No." Everyone turned to look at her. "I mean, there's no way that it would work. An AI can't control their host."

"I would have to develop the technology, but I do think it's possible," Hatch said. "I just never thought about the idea before." He gave Knox an unreadable look.

"Well, if you create the tech and Julianna is okay with sharing Pip, I'd be down for such an upgrade," Eddie stated with a broad smile on his face. He'd been warming to the idea of having an AI in his head. He'd thought about it often since being upgraded. He looked at Julianna with a question in his eyes. "What do you think?"

"Yeah, I don't care. Why would I?" Julianna stated flatly, but turned abruptly to look at one of the nearest cars—a blue 1966 Corvette convertible.

"This is all just conjecture right now." Hatch threw a tentacle in the air and waved it around, "since I'd have to develop the technology. But it does make another good argument for recruiting a Chief Engineer. I can't be expected to do everything, and Gunner is only one man."

Hatch stated that last part as if *he* wasn't. The Londil did seem to do the work of four.

Eddie cleared his throat. "Okay, all that aside for now, we've come to discuss these classified Federation storage facilities and their contents."

Julianna was grateful for the change of topic. *Pip in Eddie's head, and able to control his body?* The ideas were insane, and yet she didn't have a good reason to oppose the notions. Pip was *her* AI and maybe she didn't want to share him. Maybe she was afraid of how it would blur the boundaries. There were too many things about the idea that bothered her indirectly. She turned away from the car she'd been pretending to inspect and rejoined the conversation.

"We have the locations of the two different facilities," Julianna began, "but we were hoping you could tell us what's inside them. That will help us to determine which one to search first for the Saverus."

"Why not put eyes on both facilities?" Knox asked, and again he looked down immediately after cutting in as if ashamed of his outburst.

He was full of good questions today, although his first had almost earned him a punch in the face from Julianna. *Pip controlling her body...the idea was so strange.*

Eddie shook his head. "We just don't have the staff for that kind of thing."

"Not to mention that the facilities are at opposite ends of the galaxy," Julianna stated.

"And I'm guessing that General Reynolds is limiting this to Ghost Squadron," Hatch conjectured.

"You guessed correctly," Eddie said. "The General

believes the fewer who know about the facilities and the Saverus, the better."

"We need to cut the Saverus off at the pass, so what can you tell us about the storage facilities?" Julianna asked.

Hatched rubbed his many chins with one of his tentacles. "Well, I think I can make your job fairly easy. The storage containers are named Area Eight and Area One-Twenty-Six. The first one houses specialized weapons that the Federation created. There are other things in the facility—strange things that were too important to destroy, but too dangerous to allow out there. Some are still being studied."

"And Area One-Twenty-Six?" Julianna asked.

Hatch peered down at the goggles in his tentacle. "No weapons there, just the strangest of the strange. Many of the closets contain devices I created that were too dangerous to use. Experiments that went wrong."

"Do you know of anything the Saverus would want to get their hands on?" Eddie asked.

"Don't you mean tails?" Pip laughed.

Hatch thought for a moment. "Honestly, I've created thousands of things. I'm biased, but I thought that most of them were valuable. I can't fathom which of my extraordinary inventions a race of shapeshifters would want."

"Then I vote we go to Area Eight first. Most evil masterminds want weapons," Eddie said.

Julianna agreed with a nod, although her gut told her that this species of shapeshifters wasn't the "destroy and conquer" type. They wanted something, but it was unclear what.

Hatch lifted the goggles to his face and peered through them.

"So besides allowing you to see what's behind you, what do those fancy goggles do?" Eddie asked.

Hatch's face brightened slightly, as if he were glad to finally be asked the question. "When you encounter a Saverus you're going to need a way to penetrate its disguise, since they can look exactly like anyone else."

"Do those do that?" Julianna asked, incredibly impressed. They'd known who they were up against for only a day, and Hatch had already been working on a solution.

His bright expression faded and he shook his head. "Unfortunately they don't work—not yet. They will be able to show you a Saverus in its pure form even when it's impersonating someone, but first I'm going to need something."

"A rare crystal from a distant pirate-infested planet?" Eddie asked with mock sincerity.

"Supplies from a lava planet overrun with dangerous Kezzin?" Julianna pretended to ask, thinking of the Brotherhood base they had invaded.

"How about a scientist on Onyx Station who is being hunted by deadly mercenaries?" Knox asked, joining the game.

Hatch didn't look impressed as he shook his head. "No, none of that. What I need is quite simple."

"Oh, well that's a relief, boss. What is it?" Eddie asked.

"I need a blood sample from a Saverus," Hatch stated with a wicked smile.

7

Alpha-line Q-Ship, Federation Border Station Seven Airspace

"'Quite simple.' Isn't that Londil cute?" Eddie asked, following Julianna in as she prepared to dock. They'd been discussing the last conversation with Hatch during the trip.

"Yes, so if we see a Saverus—who could look like anyone else—we just walk up to it and ask for a sample of its blood, right?" Lars asked, joining in the laughter.

"Maybe we knock one out," Julianna said over the comm. "Marilla said that when Saverus are unconscious they return to their original form."

"You heard that, Lieutenant," Eddie replied with a chuckle, looking over his shoulder at Fletcher, who was in the back of the Q-Ship. "Have your team knock out everyone we see on this station."

"What about the scales that were found at Jaslene Corporation?" Fletcher asked. "Couldn't that be used instead of a blood sample?"

"Nope, Hatch was pretty clear that he needed a fresh blood sample to make the goggles work," Eddie stated.

"Speaking of that, isn't Jaslene Corporation located here?" Lars asked. "How come they put Area Eight here too?"

"Well, no one is supposed to know that it is," Julianna said. "I reviewed the blueprints, and the facility is hidden. Official records don't even show that it exists."

"I heard a rumor that if you don't know you're looking for it, you can't see it," one of Fletcher's soldiers said in a conspiratorial voice.

Julianna sighed. "That's ridiculous."

"I'm not so sure. There's a psychological theory that you have to see something to believe it," Lars said.

"Well, obviously something protects Area Eight from spying eyes," Eddie stated over the comm, initiating a soft dock to the station. Once the connection was secure, he proceeded to hard-dock. When the docking mechanisms were sealed, he gave the crew an all-clear.

Eddie rose, strapping his pistol into his harness. Fletcher's team were the first to file through the connector into the corridor of Federation Border Station Seven.

Lars gave Eddie a questioning look. "So they're looking for Saverus. What exactly are *we* looking for?"

"Because we like to keep it interesting, we have no fucking clue," Eddie said with a wink.

Julianna strode past the line of Special Forces soldiers with

Eddie at her side. They halted at the security checkpoint and presented their access badges.

The security guard, an older man with wiry gray hair and troubled eyes, scanned the badges. General Reynolds had arranged their clearances, although it could never be tied directly to him.

"Which way to Area Eight?" she asked the man when he handed back her badge.

His thick eyebrows knitted together. "Area what?"

"Area Eight? It's a storage facility somewhere on this station," Julianna explained.

"I've worked on this station for most of my life, and I'm not aware of an Area Eight," the security man stated. "Are you certain you're in the right place?"

"I think this just confirms that we are," Eddie said, motioning Julianna past the security checkpoint. Fletcher's men followed, and Lars brought up the rear.

I've found Area Eight, Pip informed her.

You're talking to me again?

No, not really—just for mission purposes.

I think I'm the first person to actually have an AI mad at them.

I got annoyed at the captain one time for showing off. Then there was the occasion when Lars was chewing with his mouth open. Oh, and Chester! He plays his music too loudly. I haven't found too many flaws in Marilla, but I'm still looking because—

Can we focus?

Hey, I'm sharing my interpersonal experiences with you.

I'm not your shrink.

No, but if you were I'd tell you to work on your bedside manner.

We'll get you counseling.

Good, because as the staff grows, I'm increasingly annoyed. Fletcher whistles all the time, and—

It's a relief that you found Area Eight, Julianna stated, cutting Pip off again. *I was starting to wonder how we'd find it otherwise.*

Yes, what's strange is that I've reviewed the blueprints for this station many times and have never seen Area Eight. However, this time it was there, as plain as day.

I reviewed the blueprints too, before the mission, and didn't see it.

You scanned static plans. A picture. I pulled up the blueprints directly from the station's mainframe. I'm guessing that they really do shift based on the observer.

How is that possible?

It's based on the observer effect. I'm guessing that there's something quite bizarre in Area Eight and Area One-Twenty-Six. Some real hocus-pocus that's responsible for the plans shifting.

That's very strange.

"Pip has located Area Eight," Julianna said, turning to Eddie.

"I figured you two were chatting, based on the range of looks that just crossed your face," Eddie said with a relieved smile.

"Yes, well, it would appear that Area Eight is in fact protected by some strange science," she said as Fletcher and Lars joined them. Julianna almost smiled when the Special Forces Lieutenant ambled up whistling.

"Do you want me to send my guys in first?" Fletcher asked.

Julianna nodded. She could see the real blueprints as Pip projected them in her retinal area and based on the image, there was a likely place for weapons. "There're two entrances into Area Eight. Have your team take the one on the base level at Sector 12."

Fletcher didn't hesitate before saluting sharply and pivoting to his team.

Julianna continued down the corridor with Eddie and Lars on her heels and wove her way through multiple intersecting areas, finally coming to a set of double doors. The placard beside the door clearly read **Area Eight**.

"I thought the Federation was trying to hide this place?" Lars asked, pointing his long finger at the sign.

"You can only see it because you already know about Area Eight and you're looking for it," Julianna explained.

"Because *that* makes total sense," Eddie said with a smirk.

Julianna shook her head. "It doesn't make any sense. I've never seen Federation technology like this, which makes me think what we'll find inside might blow our minds."

"You sent Fletcher's team down to the lower level based on what? Did you see something that indicated they should go down there rather than here?" Eddie asked curiously.

Julianna scanned her badge over the reader next to the door. "I saw on the schematics that the lower level has larger storage units, which made me think that weapons are housed down there. It appears that this is research and development up here, mostly smaller lab units."

The scanner buzzed once and the automatic double doors slid open to reveal a darkened hallway. The only light was a bright turquoise glow from the windows lining both sides of the corridor.

"I think we've officially entered the twilight zone," Eddie said, stepping forward.

Eddie's nose twitched from the sharp astringent smell in the air. He held in a sneeze, but Lars wasn't as successful and sneezed loudly in the eerily silent space. He looked up at Eddie and Julianna like he'd done something wrong.

"Yeah, there are definitely chemicals in the air," Julianna said, trying to put Lars at ease.

The strange glow from the laboratory units called to Eddie, making him want to press his face to the glass like a kid at an aquarium. He found that without realizing it he'd strode forward and put out his hand toward a sliding door.

"Good idea. Let's divide up," Julianna said from behind him. "I'll check this room. Lars, you take the next. Let's meet out here in five."

Eddie nodded absentmindedly, trying to make out the green orb floating in the middle of the clear case in the room ahead of him. He opened the door and walked past the computer terminals and lab equipment, halting only inches from the case.

The orb, he realized when he got closer, was covered in

a slimy green substance which dripped from the orb, stretching a few inches before springing back into place.

Eddie was surprised to find that the case was unlocked, and he stared around the deserted room to check that no one was watching his next move. This ball of slime didn't seem like the kind of thing the Saverus were after. *Who would steal a ball of gunk?* However, it was incredibly fascinating to him all the same.

On opening the case, Eddie nearly coughed from the gust of air that blasted his face. A burst of lightning sparked inside the green gob and he blinked at it, trying to understand what it was as sparks continued to fire from the middle of the ball. It reminded Eddie of neural networks in the brain sparking when a connection was made.

A thick bit of slime extended from the ball, forming a tentacle of sorts. Eddie found himself reaching out, but paused before making contact.

This was insane. He knew better than to touch unknown things. He shook his head, pulling his hand back.

Before he could shut the case again the tentacle detached from the orb and launched itself at Eddie. He threw up his arms to shield, and the goop stuck to the back of his hand. Expecting pain or some strange reaction, Eddie lowered his hand and looked at the green slime. It didn't hurt and it was neither cold nor hot, but rather it felt like nothing. He wouldn't even have known anything was stuck to him if he wasn't seeing it with his own eyes.

Eddie turned his hand over and flicked it, but the slime stayed attached. He hesitated, hovering the fingers of his other hand over the slime. *I'll just peel it off like a band-aid. Fast and painless,* he thought.

Greetings, a neutral voice said in his head as bright purple sparks shot though the large ball in the case.

"What? Who's that?" Eddie said aloud.

I haven't been given a name.

Eddie lifted his hand to his eyes and stared at the green slime. "Is that you talking in my head?"

Technically it's me talking—the host in the center of this room.

Eddie stared at the green slime on his hand. "And this? What is this?"

That is one of my agents.

"Is that how you are speaking to me telepathically?"

I'm a highly intelligent being, and that's *why I can speak to you telepathically, but to simplify matters, an agent does serve as a conductor for long-range communications.*

"That's what the agents are for?" Eddie asked.

The orb glowed and then dimmed. *No, they are spies.*

"Spies," Eddie mused. "So they can stick almost anywhere and send back intel to you?"

And I relay it to my client. Also, note that you don't need to speak aloud as long as I've established a connection with you and I'm in close proximity.

Otherwise I'd need one of these agents? Eddie asked.

A conductor. And that is correct.

Eddie shivered from the strangeness of this all. Was this how it felt to have an AI in your head? He liked it more than he had thought he would.

You were created by the Federation, is that right? Eddie asked.

Again you are correct.

Eddie scratched his head with the hand that wasn't covered in slime. *Were you difficult to create?*

That is the question you are ostensibly asking, but my higher-level sensibility tells me that's not the question you want the answer to.

Eddie's eyes widened and he stared at the green goop as it dripped again, this time stretching straight toward him. He expected it to detach from its host and land on him again. *You're correct. I was wondering if the Federation could make more like you.*

Because?

Because I work for a rogue squadron that serves the Federation.

And you could benefit from employing a spy such as myself? Is that right?

Well, and I'd get huge kudos from the Commander.

The whole blob shot forward, landing in Eddie's hands. The sphere it had covered, Eddie now could see, was a metal ball. The goop dripped through his fingers, almost too difficult to keep together. The slime on his hand joined its host, and the substance glowed.

Is this your way of telling me you want to join us?

I was created to assist the Federation. If that's what you intend, then I should accompany you.

Great. Now I just have one question.

You will find a carrying container in the cabinet to your right.

Damn, you're one smart...thing.

8

Area Eight, Federation Border Station Seven

Penrae straightened and pushed her thick glasses up the bridge of her nose. The strange contraptions were uncomfortable and sat crookedly on her face. The Saverus had taken the appearance of a lab technician she'd met upon entering the storage facility.

"Tell us where it is," Verdok encouraged, gripping Cheng's arm. He'd taken the appearance of the wiry-haired security guard from the station checkpoint.

Although the elders and the council had entrusted Verdok with this mission, Penrae doubted his strategy. Bringing Cheng along had been risky. The old scientist had lost his mind long before they abducted him. She did understand, however, that locating the Tangle Thief without Cheng's help might be difficult. Not completely impossible, but risky enough that Verdok had insisted on bringing him along.

"I don't re-re-remember," Cheng stuttered, shaking as

he combed his fingers through his white-streaked black hair.

"You're lying," Verdok said in a terse whisper.

"Maybe he really doesn't know." Penrae pulled her glasses off her face, but quickly replaced them. Okay, the scientist she'd shapeshifted into needed the spectacles to see. She'd just have to deal with them.

Verdok shot a disgusted look at her, which was almost worse than when he was in his original form. Humans had so many expressions on their wrinkled faces. "He knows—we've already established that. He just has to remember. Which unit holds the Tangle Thief?"

Verdok tightened his grip on Cheng's arm and led him down the dark corridor. The only light, a bright blue glow, came from the windows of the laboratory rooms. "Think. Think. Think. Where is the Tangle Thief located?"

Cheng slid both his hands over his hollow cheeks. "I can't hear anything over the noise."

Penrae pulled in a breath. The scientist was soon to be useless. Usually he heard "the noise" before he passed out, and then he'd be unconscious for hours. "Verdok, why don't you let me try?"

Verdok swiveled his gaze to her, his hostility fierce. "Fine, but get him to talk. We're running out of time." She tried not to appear as flustered at she felt, but it was harder when she had shapeshifted and wasn't used to this person's face.

Penrae stepped forward, patting Cheng on the back. "Dr. Sung, you're all right. We're here to help you. All we need is the location for the Tangle Thief. If you can help us find it, we can fix you."

The doctor looked up at Penrae with hope in his eyes. "You think you can fix me?"

She nodded, smiling broadly. "All we need is the Tangle Thief."

Deep lines creased the man's brow. "But it's the Tangle Thief that made me like this." He shook his head, suddenly more upset than before. "No, the Tangle Thief is bad. Bad. Bad. *Bad!*"

Penrae grabbed Cheng's hands before he began stomping his feet, steering him over to a wall. "If we have the device, we can reverse the process," she lied.

Cheng froze, staring at the white floor. He knotted his hands into his thick beard. "Reverse the process..."

"Yes," Penrae said in a soothing voice. "We want to help you."

Cheng probably wasn't sure who she was. The poor scientist saw a different person every time he looked at his captors, so he obviously didn't know who to trust. She hoped he believed she was a Federation scientist. That would make this easier.

"You want to help me?" he asked feebly.

She nodded. It felt strange to have a neck and arms and legs. "That's right. We just need your cooperation."

Cheng pressed into the wall, which was lined with windows. In the laboratory room was an empty case, and a row of computers and cabinets. Area Eight was an incredibly strange place, Penrae sensed.

"Will you keep those large snakes away from me?" Cheng asked. He reached out and gripped her hand. "Please?"

Penrae exchanged an uncomfortable look with

Verdok, who was no doubt ready to explode. Instead she pressed her other hand over Cheng's. "Of course. We're going to catch the Saverus who abducted you. Don't worry, we'll make sure that they pay. All you have to do is tell me where the Tangle Thief is located. It's here, isn't it?"

With a renewed sense of hope, Cheng looked around the facility. "Here? Hmmmm?"

Verdok let out an impatient sigh.

"He's thinking," Penrae whispered to him. Her partner's hot temper was going to ruin everything, and then it was going to be *her* fault. She always took the blame, because it was easier that way. Verdok would find a way to sabotage her behind the scenes unless she took responsibility.

"This is Area One-Twenty-Six?" Cheng asked, spinning in a complete circle.

"Damn it, no!" Verdok yelled, his old face flushing red.

Penrae stepped in front of him. "What he meant to say is that this is Area Eight. Remember, you indicated that this was where the Tangle Thief was stored?"

Penrae forced a sympathetic smile onto her face. Of course, by "indicated" she meant the insane doctor had grunted and thrown a shaking hand at the records that had been stolen from Jaslene Corporation when they'd presented them to him. She had especially felt sorry for him that day. No one should have to undergo interrogation for so many hours. That was when Verdok had lost his temper—yet again—and shifted to his original form, and seeing the giant snake had scared Cheng enough that he had indicated Area Eight was where they should go. Verdok knew they weren't supposed to show their original form to outsiders. It was a rule of the council. That form was sacred...for some reason.

"Area Eight..." Cheng pulled at his salt and pepper beard, his eyes off in thought.

"Sir," a voice called from the entrance to Area Eight. Sark entered and ran in their direction. The Petigren's clawed feet tapped against the floor as he scurried over.

That was another part of the plan Penrae had been against. She didn't understand why the Petigrens had to accompany them. Sneaking onto the Federation Border Station had been difficult enough. Smuggling in the rat people had been exponentially more complicated. However, the elders thought the Petigren species should always serve them. They didn't realize that this species, who would sacrifice themselves for the Saverus, were going to be their downfall. The elders weren't happy unless something was dying to protect them.

Verdok whipped around to face the smaller creature. "What is it, Sark?"

"We have a disturbance on the lower level. There's a military force sweeping the area," Sark told him.

"What? That area was supposed to be clear," Verdok said, his voice vibrating.

"These don't appear to be Federation soldiers," Sark informed them, his beady eyes looking between Penrae and Verdok.

"Pirates, then. They've probably come to steal, and will take off with the Tangle Thief if we don't stop them," Verdok at once assumed.

"Or they could be—" Penrae began.

Verdok cut her off and spoke to Sark. "Attack them. If

nothing else, your battle will serve as a distraction so we can get out of here."

Sark nodded obediently, backing up to the exit. "Yes, sir. Thank you for the chance to sacrifice myself for you."

Verdok didn't give Sark any more of his attention. Instead he turned back to Cheng, who was muttering equations under his breath.

"Where is the Tangle Thief? I'm running out of time," Verdok said, frustration in his voice.

He's *running out of time*, Penrae thought bitterly. Yes, because when they got the Tangle Thief he was going to take the credit. She should have realized that from the beginning.

Cheng held up his hands and began counting on his fingers the way a child would. He lifted a single finger, then raised two fingers on his other hand. "One and two and then..." Cheng held up three fingers on each hand.

"One-twenty-six?" Verdok yelled. "Are you telling me we are in the wrong place?"

"No," Cheng said, staring intently at his shaking hands. "But we are. Area Eight is not where the Tangle Thief is located."

"What? Are you serious?" Verdok said, shoving Cheng hard into the wall.

Cheng appeared unflustered by the assault and stared around the facility as if seeing it for the first time. He chuckled. "Oh, no. This is definitely not where it is. I remember now. This is *my* unit. *His* storage unit was Area One-Twenty-Six."

"Your unit?" Penrae asked, suddenly confused. Every

now and then the scientist sounded lucid when he spoke, sparks of his old intelligence shining through.

Verdok grunted. "You moronic human! You told us it was—"

The sound of running footsteps interrupted Verdok, and the three looked up in unison as two distant figures sped into view and halted in the hallway ahead.

9

Area Eight, Federation Border Station Seven

"Teach?" Julianna said, her voice cautious. "What's in the box?"

Eddie held up the plastic box he was carrying with both hands. "This is the reason you're going to call me a genius."

"I think you'll need a bigger box for that," Julianna said dryly. She and Lars had already searched most of the rooms on this corridor before Eddie surfaced from the first.

"Seriously, it's really cool. I'll explain later," he replied as they rounded into a second hallway. More rooms filled with glowing blue light lined the long corridor.

"Do you think it's safe to remove something from here?" she asked.

"Yes. I sort of asked permission," Eddie explained, clumsily sticking the box under one arm.

"Sort of?" Julianna shook her head. "I'm afraid to ask."

"I found a small box in one of the rooms," Lars said.

"After a few seconds it morphed into a second box, then a third. It continued to do that until it shrank back into just the one." He shook his head. "It was incredibly strange, but seemingly useless for our purposes."

Julianna agreed with a nod. "Yeah, I found a bunch of jars with brains in them in my first room. You absolutely don't want to know what was in the second room. And the third was empty, but I did hear voices in there."

"Hearing voices, eh?" Eddie asked, peeking into a room.

"I'm still not sure what we should be looking for," Lars said, sticking his head into a different lab area.

"Anything that someone would want to steal." Julianna eyed the box under Eddie's arm. "Is that what you found?"

He shook his head. "I don't think an alien population would go to such lengths for this. It's mostly something we'll benefit from. The Saverus either want a weapon or something that's incredibly useful."

"Right," Julianna said, turning back to the open room. She strode into the mostly empty space, wondering if she would find anything worthwhile.

"What? Are you serious?" A voice boomed down the hallway.

Julianna reversed out of the room, meeting Eddie and Lars in the hallway. They exchanged uncertain looks.

From their original direction she heard, "You moronic human!"

"Come on," she whispered urgently, sprinting back the way they'd come.

Eddie shoved the box with the green blob into Lars' hands. The Kezzin, being larger, handled it easily and didn't complain about carrying it. Pulling his pistol, Eddie ran in the direction of the voices.

Leaving Lars behind, he and Julianna quickly made it to the intersection of the hallways and halted, taking in the strange sight at the far end of the corridor. The security guard who had scanned their badges had a strange-looking man pressed against one of the walls. The man's head, which was covered in long black hair, lolled forward. He appeared to be unconscious as he slid to the deck.

The security guard faced Eddie and Julianna, who approached guardedly. The man gave the woman beside him an uncertain look. She wore a white lab coat and black glasses.

"What are you two doing here?" the security guard asked.

"I thought you didn't know where Area Eight was," Julianna called. The pair were roughly ten yards from the man.

"I asked you a question. What are you doing down here?" the security guard asked, flexing his hand over the weapon on his belt. The woman beside him backed up several paces.

"Did you find Area Eight after we said something to you?" Julianna asked.

There was something different about the security guard. He appeared as he had before, but any warmth was gone. It was as if he were a shell.

Oh fuck! Eddie halted, aiming his weapon at the man as

his eyes darted to the passed-out man on the ground. *What was going on here? These had to be them!*

"It's a Sav—" Eddie didn't finish his sentence, because at precisely that moment the two figures shifted before their very eyes. The security guard morphed into a mirror image of Eddie and the woman grew in height and changed her appearance until she looked exactly like Julianna.

The Saverus darted out the exit. Julianna and Eddie sprinted after them. Once through the double doors, Eddie realized that one had gone right and the other left.

"I'll take the left," Eddie said, sprinting after the figure who looked exactly like him. However, he was proud to say that the imposter didn't have his speed or grace. When he'd caught up with the racing man Eddie halted, lifting his weapon and firing once. The Saverus jerked to the right, as if hit. Feeling a momentary victory, Eddie strode down the hallway to the figure of himself, who was clutching the wall.

With his weapon still out, he approached slowly. "Hands up there, buddy." It was strange to talk to himself disrespectfully. *This was a mind game, though,* he admitted to himself.

Although Eddie had thought that the Saverus had been shot, he didn't see any blood. Then the alien pulled the pistol from his holster and fired in Eddie's direction, missing entirely. He stumbled after firing the weapon, but straightened and continued down a hallway to the right.

Damn it, Eddie thought. He shouldn't have let the Saverus get off any shots, but it was distracting to walk up to himself believing he'd shot himself.

Eddie rounded the corner and halted. The short

hallway was empty, and it split in two different directions. Cautiously and with weapon at the ready Eddie approached, sliding against the wall. He slipped around the corner, pistol first. The hallway was vacant. He spun around. Again nothing.

What the fuck? Where had he gone? This section of the Border Station was a confusing mess of intersecting tunnels and narrow corridors. It was a maze with so many places to hide.

Hearing footsteps at his back, Eddie swung around. He hesitated as Julianna bolted into the far end of the hallway some fifteen yards away.

Wait. Maybe Julianna, maybe a sniveling shapeshifter.

Eddie kept his pistol at the ready and his eyes intently focused on Julianna, who was regarding him with the same skepticism.

Fletcher stood vigilantly at the far end of the darkened corridor. *There was something not right about this place.* It wasn't the absence of light or the nukes they'd found behind seemingly impenetrable glass. This seemed like the armory the Federation had taken from the bad aliens and was keeping safe. Fletcher liked that idea, but he didn't like the scratching sounds he kept hearing overhead.

"Sir?" Kendrick called, recapturing Fletcher's attention.

He turned to his surveillance specialist. "What is it?"

He motioned to an open storage facility ahead. "That door is open."

"And?" Fletcher asked.

"All the rest were locked," Kendrick imparted.

He was right. They hadn't entered any of the units, only peered through the glass to see the contents.

Fletcher motioned to the soldier beside Kendrick. "You and Nona go check it out."

The rest of the team had divided up to search this part of Area Eight, which was large and spread-out. The enclosed hallways did nothing to make Fletcher feel any better. He felt boxed in, like a sardine in a can. If something happened, there were a million places to run and no good places for cover.

Scratch. Scratch. Scratch.

Fletcher looked up, listening to the incessant scratching. What was it? The tiled ceiling vibrated slightly, as if something had run across it. Was it possible that Border Station Seven had rats?

Fletcher shivered in disgust. He'd spent enough time in trenches and old buildings to have a thorough hatred for rats. Those fuckers had chewed through the explosives that were supposed to put a swift halt to a battle with a gang of dangerous pirates, so it had been their fault that the pirates got away. And that was the same band of pirates who had supposedly taken out his father's squadron. Once again Rosco's gang had gotten away and vengeance had slipped through Fletcher's fingers. One day that would change. One day he'd avenge his father.

The words that rang in his head during every mission played now. "Keep your chin up, eyes open, and mouth shut." Fletcher's father's words always came to him when he needed them most.

He halted. Raised his chin. Peered at the ceiling as it rattled louder than before. *Something was wrong.*

Taking several steps backward, Fletcher recoiled when he saw what spilled out in front of him.

Simultaneously, something hairy dove out of the storage unit at Nona and Kendrick as another creature dropped from the ceiling. Fletcher clamped his mouth shut as the alien rose from the floor. It was a man, but...not a man. The creature had patches of hair on his face. Whiskers. Pointy teeth. And...a fucking tail. It was a rat-man.

Although a foot shorter than Fletcher, the rat-man looked powerful as it dove at him. Fletcher rolled out from underneath the assault and whipped around, bringing the butt of his rifle down hard on the head of the beast. It screeched loudly.

Behind him, Fletcher heard a similar assault and shrieking as Nona and Kendrick battled their own rat-men.

The alien rolled over and crawled in the direction of Fletcher's feet. His hands had long clawed fingers and they scratched at the deck. The monster was faster on all fours, making it to Fletcher's feet in no time. Fletcher viciously kicked the creature, grimacing at the skull's crunch. It reminded him of when he'd lived in a back alley for a week on a covert mission. This time it was worse, though.

Fletcher kicked the small rat-man to the side after he stilled. There were two more of the aliens at Nona and Kendrick's feet, their rodent eyes wide and staring life-lessly at the ceiling.

"Good work. Search the rest of this area," Fletcher ordered. "It appears we have an infestation."

Julianna aimed her gun at her partner. It was the strangest experience. They were supposed to work together. Die to protect each other if necessary. How was she pointing her gun straight at Eddie? Or *not* Eddie...

He similarly had his gun pointed unflinchingly at her. The figure of herself she'd been racing after had shifted rapidly through three other forms and spilled through a crowd of scientists filing in the opposite direction. Then Julianna had lost her. But here was Eddie. Or whoever.

"Julianna, it's me," Eddie said, his eyes sharp.

"That's what an imposter would say," Julianna retorted.

"Well, how am I supposed to know it's you? I saw that Saverus take your identity too. *You* might be the imposter," Eddie said.

"I'm not a Saverus. I'm..." Julianna's voice trailed away. How was she going to convince Eddie it was actually her? And how was he going to convince *her*?

"Tell me something that only you know," Eddie said, glancing over his shoulder. She did the same. They couldn't leave themselves wide-open for an attack.

The adrenaline of the moment overwhelmed her. How was she supposed to think while holding her partner at gunpoint and having a weapon pointed at her?

"What do you want to know?" she finally asked.

"Damn it, Jules, come up with something." Tension gripped Eddie's face. This was stressful for him too, but neither could be trusted until they were proved to be the real person. And if he couldn't? Was Julianna going to shoot Eddie? The idea filled her stomach with disgust.

Give me something, Pip.

Tell him that he chews on his lip when he's thinking.

For fuck's sake, that's not a real specific trait.

It's true, though. Also, he waits until everyone in the crew is eating before taking his first bite.

Seriously, are you intentionally trying to be unhelpful?

These are genuine observations that no one else can make of the captain.

I'm looking for information—something I would know. Something about Ghost Squadron! Julianna's mind was all over the place. She could say something about Hatch or one of the missions or the Q-Ships, but they didn't really know how the Saverus worked. Maybe they had access to more than just a person's appearance. She wanted to give Eddie something that irrefutably told him she was the real Julianna.

Tell him you know that he's hiding a demon about his parents.

I can't. I'm not ready, and he's not ready to talk about it.

But that's one thing you know that no one does. He's hinted at it.

And I'm not throwing it in his face right now, Julianna yelled back at Pip.

Eddie lowered his weapon with a strange expression on his face.

"What? What are you doing?" Julianna asked, looking at him with shock.

"It's you," he said with a sigh. "I know it is."

"How?" she asked, her weapon still pointed at him.

"That look on your face. You always get it when you're talking to Pip. Only the real Julianna would have a conversation with Pip when she was being held at gunpoint," Eddie said, and to her surprise he laughed.

Julianna didn't know what to do. Maybe she should stand her ground? Then she realized Eddie had given her all the proof she needed. Only the real Eddie would recognize the subtle nuances that happened to her face when she spoke with Pip. She lowered her weapon and let out a relieved breath.

"It's really you?" she asked, unnerved by having to chase herself and aim a weapon at Eddie.

"It's really me, and all I wish right now is that I could still get wasted once we return to *Ricky Bobby*," Eddie said with a wide smile.

It really *was* Eddie. Why had it been so hard to prove themselves to each other when it was actually very easy?

That's the paradox of most relationships, Julianna, Pip said in her head. **We can be ourselves, but still hide who we truly are. All we have to do is be honest with one another, and yet too often we hide who we are in our silence.**

Shut up, Pip.

10

Interrogation Chamber, *Ricky Bobby*, Tangki System

Lars hadn't just brought back the white container with the green goop, he'd also found the man the Saverus had been intimidating. Lars had the good sense to realize the man probably knew something, and had led him to the Q-Ship.

Julianna had worried initially that the man was a Saverus, but he hadn't shifted and hadn't try to flee like the other two. He mostly babbled to himself.

"Has he said anything of use?" Eddie asked Lars at the door to the interrogation room.

The Kezzin shook his head. "He just keeps counting. I think he's up to a hundred thousand."

Eddie shot Julianna a look of disbelief. "Impressive."

"Or a big waste of time," she said. "Did we just bring a certifiably insane person aboard the ship?"

"Don't you mean *another* certifiably insane person?" Eddie swiveled his head playfully. "We're all mad here."

"Did you just quote Lewis Carroll?" Lars asked, surprised.

"I did." Eddie pressed a proud hand to his chest and bowed slightly. "Chester loaned me a copy of *Alice's Adventures in Wonderland*. Said he was named after the cat."

"Watch out," Lars said from the corner of his mouth in Julianna's direction. "The captain is getting cultured."

"Don't you worry, I still like my meat rare and my music loud," Eddie said with a chuckle.

Julianna rolled her eyes. "I fail to see what the temperature of meat or the volume of music has to do with being cultured or not."

"That's an excellent point, dear Julianna," Eddie said in a distinguished voice. "I do apologize for making an illogical correlation."

She shook her head and opened the door to the interrogation room. The "guest," as they were calling him since he was nonviolent and seemed mostly content to be aboard, was sitting on the floor with his legs crossed. He had a thick head of shoulder-length black hair, which was streaked with white. His beard was unkempt, and his brown eyes buzzed with tension. The man was underfed, and wore dingy clothes that hung loosely on his lanky frame.

His fingers popped up as he counted. "One hundred thousand and twenty-four. One hundred thousand and twenty-five. One hundred thousand and twenty-six." The man dropped his hands into his lap and looked up at them serenely. "Oh, that was nice. Shall we begin again? One, two, three, four—"

"Actually, can we pause the counting for a moment?" Eddie asked.

The man gaped, like that was the most ridiculous idea he'd heard all day. He was definitely bonkers.

Julianna motioned to the chair on the other side of the table. "Would you like to take a seat?"

As if this were another crazy question they were asking him, the guest pushed back into the steel wall of the room with offense on his face.

"Okay…" Julianna said, her voice tentative. Cautiously she approached him and squatted so they were at eye level. This wasn't the tough-girl act she put on in battle—this was one Eddie hadn't seen before. *The woman of a hundred faces*, he mused.

"I'm Commander Fregin and this is…" She held out her hand, indicating Eddie.

"Captain Teach," Eddie said on cue.

"You can call me 'Julianna,'" she said, her voice soft.

"Julianna," the man repeated, seeming to practice the name.

"Yes, and what can we call you?" she asked.

The man's bright eyes darted up from his hands and straight at Julianna. "Name… What did they call me?"

"The Saverus? Is that who you mean?" Julianna asked.

At the mention of the aliens, the man recoiled. So he hadn't enjoyed his time with them, which Eddie had suspected was the case.

"It's okay," Julianna said. "You're safe now. They can't get to you. We have you protected."

The man relaxed a bit and looked up at Eddie. When

their eyes connected the captain had the briefest moment of déjà vu, as if they'd met before.

"What's your name, buddy? Do you remember?" Eddie asked.

"Lo-Lo-Cheng," he stuttered.

Julianna straightened from her crouch, giving Eddie a tense look. She was probably thinking the same thing as him. If it took this long to get the man's name out of him, finding out anything of use was going to take forever.

"Cheng, why did the Sav—" Eddie stopped himself. They needed to keep this guy as steady as possible. "Why were you at Area Eight?"

The man gulped several times like his mouth was dry, so Julianna disappeared out the door, returning a moment later with a glass of water. Cheng was panting now, and obviously dehydrated.

He took the water, downed the entire glass, and handed it back to Julianna with a hopeful expression. She nodded and left again.

"Device," Cheng said, wiping the back of his hand across mouth. He looked somehow more lucid when Julianna returned a moment later with another glass of water and a canteen for refills. She also placed a plate of dried meat and fruit in front of him, offering him a reassuring smile.

"Thank you," he managed to say around the glass pressed to his cracked lips.

"Device? They took you there hoping you could help them find a device? Is that right?" Eddie guessed.

Cheng crammed a handful of dried cherries into his mouth and nodded.

"Why would you know where this device is?" Julianna asked, kneeling again by their guest.

"I built it," he said with his mouth full.

Julianna looked up at Eddie, eagerness in her expression. They were getting closer.

"You built it? What is this device?" Eddie asked.

Cheng picked up the glass and nearly took a bath when he took his next sip, spilling half its contents down his front. "Actually, I helped build it."

"What is it?" Julianna asked, her voice a bit more forceful. They were so close.

Cheng shook his head adamantly, his black hair whipping him in the face. "No one should have the device. It's dangerous." He pushed away the empty plate and pulled his knees into his chest, suddenly shivering.

"We're trying to protect the device. That's why we were there," Julianna explained. "If you can tell us what it is and where to find it, we can put extra security on it."

This seemed to make Cheng relax a tad. "It's not at Area Eight."

"Area One-Twenty-Six, then?" Eddie asked.

Cheng jerked his head in a roundabout nod.

"Can you tell us where and what it is?" Julianna pressed.

"I don't know where. My research partner does," Cheng said.

"What is it?" Julianna tried again. She appeared to be using every bit of her patience, since Cheng was really making them work for this information.

He shook his head, pressing his mouth shut tightly.

Okay, so he wasn't going to tell them the name. Maybe if they gave them another plate of food he'd talk.

"All right…" Julianna said, drawing out the word. "This research partner—can you tell us anything about this person?"

"Londil," Cheng corrected.

"Did you say Londil? Your research partner was a Londil?" Eddie asked, straightening. What were the odds?

"Doctor A-a-a…" Cheng stuttered.

"Doctor who?" Julianna asked, desperation slipping into her voice.

"Doctor Aiden?" Cheng said mostly to himself, as if testing the name to see if it sounded right.

"'Doctor Aiden?'" Julianna repeated.

Cheng shook his head, his eyes sparking like something was suddenly clear. "No. A'Din Hatcherik!"

11

Hatch's Lab, *Ricky Bobby*, Tangki System

Julianna held onto Cheng's arm as she helped him through the corridor. He was stronger after the food and water, and now mostly seemed breathless from the excitement.

"He's here? He's really here?" Cheng kept saying. At least he wasn't counting anymore.

"See for yourself." Eddie pointed to Hatch, who was flattened out under a gray DeLorean. His tentacles were wrapped around the car, and he was also tinkering under the hood, while he simultaneously worked under the car.

"Doc, I can't find it," Knox called from the back of the lab, his black Mohawk barely visible over the top of a table of parts where he was searching.

"I told you eighty-eight times, kid!" Hatch yelled, his voice muffled under the car. "The flux capacitor is—"

Hatch froze briefly, then his tentacles retracted and he pushed out from under the car. He looked a bit distracted as he gazed at the three who approached. He whipped around and waved Knox off, his cheeks puffing out. "Never mind. Work on that ship project."

"Which one?" Knox asked, his face scrunching as he peered over the top of the workstation. When he spotted Eddie and Julianna he ducked. "Right. Ship project. You got it."

Julianna moved her hands to her hips and offered Hatch a tight smile. "What are you working on?"

"Something for the ship. And for your current mission." Hatch added the last bit, reaching over and shutting the open car door.

"We don't care if you work on your hobbies," Eddie said with a laugh.

"Hobby. Yes, that's what I'm working on." Hatch slapped the side of the car affectionately. "We're just fixing up this old DeLorean."

Julianna eyed the mechanic sideways. "Is that right?"

Hatch puffed out his cheeks and feigned an odd smile. "Yes, Julie, of course."

What are they working on? Julianna asked Pip.

How should I know? he answered.

You've been quiet for too long. I know you've been hanging out with the boys.

Then you know that as a man, I can't disclose what happens in the man cave.

Julianna ignored the "man" statement. There was no arguing with Pip on such things anymore. *Is it something dangerous?* she asked him.

Is it something dangerous! Pip repeated with a laugh and a hint of disbelief at the question.

Is it illegal?

Pip huffed. **Is it illegal? Ha!**

Repeating what I say is not answering the question.

By the way, you should stop interrogating me. Your new friend appears to be having social anxiety.

Julianna turned around to find that Cheng hadn't come all the way into the lab with them. He had stalled by the entrance, and was clutching the doorframe as if he were reconsidering this whole thing.

She trotted over and wrapped an arm around his shoulder. "Hey, Cheng. Everything is all right. You wanted to see Hatch. We've brought you to him."

"It's so bright in here. And loud," Cheng said, covering his ears and squeezing his eyes shut.

The lights in the lab *were* a bit bright, which was typical for Hatch's workspace, but aside from Eddie and Hatch discussing the car there were no other real noises. However, Cheng still seemed pained by a loud noise as he pressed his hands over his ears.

"Ricky Bobby, will you please reduce the lights?" Julianna asked.

"Of course," Ricky Bobby replied. "Lights reduced to sixty percent."

Cheng relaxed only slightly as Julianna led him over to Hatch.

Hatch was momentarily distracted by the newbie, but then his face brightened and one of his tentacles popped into the air. "Oh, I did have a chance to test and examine what you brought back."

"Yes, and what *was* in the white box?" Julianna asked, her focus rapidly shifting.

Hatch reached over to the white container, which was sitting on a nearby workstation. He opened the lid and pulled out a giant pile of green goo.

"Is that the stuff from the *Vermix Rex?*" Julianna asked, suddenly excited. They'd destroyed the last one known to be in existence, and although the giant worms were highly dangerous, their blood was literally a lifesaver.

Hatch shook his large head. "No, but it's still something extraordinary."

When he set the green goo on the work station, it congealed into a mound like gelatin and a single flash of energy shot through its center.

"Is that thing..." Julianna's voice trailed away, since she wasn't sure what the pile of goo was.

"It's alive," Hatch said triumphantly.

Eddie turned to Julianna. "It's a spy. Watch this." He pulled off a piece of the goo and stuck it on the underside of the table, then separated up another small bit from a mother source, and handed it to Julianna.

She hesitated, but after an encouraging nod from Hatch she took it.

Hello, a voice that wasn't Pip's said in her head. She knew Pip's voice like she knew her own, and this wasn't him.

"Who is that?" Julianna asked, looking from the green slime in her hand to Eddie and Hatch.

"He doesn't have a name," Hatch said, cheerfully.

"Yet," Eddie said, with promise.

The agent reports that the area is dark and approximately sixty-eight degrees, the voice said in her head again. *Within view are a wrench, a drill, and an oilcan.*

Julianna looked under the table where Eddie had stuck the other bit of goo. Sure enough, those objects were present.

There are three voices, although the agent senses that there are more beings in the vicinity, the voice said.

Julianna looked up, awe on her face. "This thing's a spy!"

Eddie smiled broadly, sliding his hands into his pockets. "Pretty cool, huh?"

"Fucking brilliant," Julianna said, pulling the piece of green slime from her hand. It came away cleanly, and when she held it close to the mound it shot out of her hand and rejoined the main source.

Thank you, the voice said in her head.

"Wait, I don't have to be connected to the...the thing for it to talk to me?" Julianna asked, looking at Hatch.

He shook his head. "It appears to have a telepathic range of approximately fifteen feet. However, Teach showed you how it was intended to be used. You place an agent where you want it to spy and then connect to it through the transmitter."

"Wow, who would have thought a blob would be so useful?" Julianna mused, staring at the thing as it pulsed with energy.

"Useful and highly intelligent," Hatch stated. "Although it's not sentient, it does have the ability to learn. It can bounce from location to location. Observe that around it and blend into its environment."

"'Bob!'" Eddie declared.

"What?" Julianna asked. "Are you blurting out random things again? I thought we had cured you of that."

"'Bob,'" Eddie repeated, pointing to the green electrified material. "Bounce, observe and blend. 'Bob the blob.'"

That name is accurate, Bob said in Julianna's head.

"I agree," Hatch said with a smile. "Accurate, and it has a ring to it."

"So we can all hear Bob, then? At the same time?" Julianna asked. This 'Bob' was something else.

"Yes, he can broadcast to anyone in the general vicinity or anyone connected to a transmitter, as I mentioned before," Hatch stated.

"Unless it is instructed to create an individual connection forged to specific agents and transmitters," Cheng said, his voice suddenly clear and his eyes gleaming as he regarded Bob.

"Yes, I was about to say that," Hatch said, astounded. "How did you know that?"

"I created Bob," Cheng stated flatly.

12

Hatch's Lab, *Ricky Bobby*, Tangki System

"What did you say?" Hatch asked, looking straight at Cheng.

Eddie stepped to Cheng's side. "When we were in Area Eight, we found—"

"Cheng?" Hatch rushed forward, squinting like he wasn't seeing him quite clearly. He was suddenly vibrating with surprise, but he stayed at a distance from the man.

Cheng nodded, sweeping his hands over his arms. "Yes, I-I-I...think that's me. When my mind clears, I remember what it was like to be who I was."

"How are we not ourselves?" Eddie said in a mused tone.

"He said that you two created a device together," Julianna interjected.

"We created many things together. Cheng was my research partner for several years." Hatch neared Cheng and looked him over. "But you died?"

"Abducted," Cheng corrected, standing as stoically as if he were in a lineup of thieves.

"By the Saverus?" Julianna guessed.

Cheng nodded.

However, Hatch didn't appear to be listening. His face was overwhelmed by his surprise and he ran a tentacle over his chin, surprise changing to awe. "This is impossible."

"Only if you believe it is," Eddie said, quoting another line from *Alice's Adventures in Wonderland*. How could he not? It had been the perfect setup.

"Right, right," Hatch said, now staring at the floor and pacing as he tried to piece things together. "It's so incredible to see you. When you disappeared, I hadn't seen you in the better part of a few years, and…"

"Yes, we had been working remotely," Cheng stated, still frozen, arms by his sides.

"Just video calls," Hatch said, nodding. "And then you just up and disappeared one day. So the Saverus—"

"Actually, no." Cheng's mouth hardly parted for the words. "I was testing our last invention."

"No!" Hatch said, his eyes wide.

Cheng hung his head, shame making his shoulders hunch. "I'm afraid so."

"But we knew that—"

"That it had flaws," Cheng said, finishing Hatch's sentence.

"And it was never intended to be used for human life." Hatch's tone now was punishing.

"I know." Cheng scratched his beard with both hands. "And I've suffered ever since from the radiation."

"What was this device?" Julianna asked. "This is what the Saverus are after, right?"

Hatch seemed to think. "Yes, that would make sense. It's a very valuable tool, and absolutely deadly no matter whose hands it is in. That was why, after Cheng's disappearance, I had the device *I* was working on placed in Area One-Twenty-Six." Hatch continued pacing, seemingly to relieve his nervous energy. "I really should have seen this coming. It all makes so much sense now."

"It might to you two," Eddie said over the clanging of metal in the back of the lab. Knox was apparently working on a project.

"This device...what is it?" Julianna asked.

"The T-T-T..." Cheng's voice trailed away, unable to finish his sentence.

"The Tangle Thief." Hatch waddled over and laid a comforting tentacle on his old friend's shoulder. "It's okay, you'll be fine."

"What does the Tangle Thief do?" Eddie asked, backing toward the workstation and pulling himself up to sit on its surface next to Bob.

Cheng seemed to come back to himself and nodded before saying, "Entanglement."

"That's right," Hatch said, encouragingly, waddling back to where he'd been pacing. "The Tangle Thief was based on the quantum theories of entanglement. There are two parts, a receiver and a client."

"Like Bob?" Eddie asked, jerking a thumb in the direction of the green blob.

Hatch nodded, his face brightening and the wrinkles around his eyes disappearing for a moment. "Yes, just like

Bob. The receiver is placed on that which is supposed to be stolen, or relocated. We never intended it to be a burglary device. It was just a clever name."

"But in the end, it stole a lot," Cheng said, a chill in his voice. The Tangle Thief, it sounded like to Eddie, had stolen this man's faculties and the better part of his life.

"That it did," Hatch said with a sympathetic nod. He was never this kind to anyone. Well, maybe Knox at times.

"What is the client's role in this?" Julianna asked, steering the discussion back on track, as she was prone to do.

"The client is placed wherever the object is to be relocated to," Hatch explained. "You see, in entanglement theory two particles are always connected, even when separated by distance."

"Again like Bob," Eddie observed.

"Yes, that's where I originally got the idea," explained Cheng. "While I was making Bob, I figured I could use the same principle to misplace an object if entanglement was established by correlating it to a particle of sorts."

Eddie noticed that when Cheng spoke of his work he was lucid, which was different from the dazed look in his eyes otherwise.

"So you put one device on a car," Eddie said motioning to the DeLorean. "Then you take the client and put it on Onyx Station and activate it, and what...the car disappears?"

"And reappears on Onyx Station," Hatch said, nodding.

"That sounds like an incredible technology," Eddie stated.

"Except that early tests showed that when used, the

Tangle Thief created tears in the universe where deadly radiation leaked through," Hatch said.

"Oh, which is why it was locked up," Eddie guessed.

Hatch puffed out his cheeks. "Destroying it would have been too dangerous. We were afraid it might have fatal repercussions."

"And you used it on yourself?" Julianna asked Cheng.

He nodded. "I'm afraid so. It worked, and then it didn't. The Tangle Thief wasn't meant to transport human life, but I didn't fully realize that until after the fact. I didn't land where the client was located, which was on the other side of my house. I found myself in a strange, deserted land. I still don't know where it was. I was holding the receiver but it was fried, meaning I wasn't going to get back. All I can figure out is that the tear I created when I transported attracted the attention of the Saverus. I know now that they'd had wind of the project and were trying to track down the device."

Hatch let out a long breath. "Good thing we had my Tangle Thief secure at Area One-Twenty-Six. We searched your house and didn't find anything. You had simply vanished. I knew the project was dangerous, so I terminated it."

Cheng clapped his hand to his forehead. "My son? He was gone?"

"Dominic?" Hatch asked, scratching the side of his head. "Yes, I'm afraid so. There were many theories. Like that you took him and disappeared. That something had happened to you both. Honestly, after the investigation came back inconclusive I had to assume you were dead." A deep regret filled Hatch's eyes. "I, of course, didn't know what to think, but believed you were gone forever."

"My son..." Cheng was lost in jumbled thoughts. His eyes were haunted, and regret surfaced and took over his expression. He combed his hand through his hair several times. "I never forgot him. Always regretted that I... But what could I do? The Saverus abducted me. I pretty much never considered I'd come back to the world. The Saverus weren't going to let me go, and they didn't give me much of a life. Mostly just endless days in a lab where they expected me to remake the Tangle Thief."

"But you didn't," Hatch guessed.

"Of course not, but not because I didn't try. I thought they'd release me if I did, but the Tangle Thief took something from me when I transported. Maybe it put my brain cells where the client was and the rest of me in the desert." Cheng laughed uncomfortably.

"But that's why the Saverus are after the other Tangle Thief now," Julianna stated.

"The one in Area One-Twenty-Six," Eddie added.

"We'll have to alert the facility," Hatch stated.

"Yes, but as we just learned, the Saverus are incredibly hard to stop. They turned into us." Julianna motioned to her and Eddie.

"Julie, you should have shot first and asked questions later," Hatch said with a morbid laugh.

"Ha, ha," Eddie said humorlessly.

"Well, at least we know what they're after," Julianna said, letting out a sigh.

"And you're back, Cheng," Hatch said excitedly. "I never thought the day would come."

"It's pretty remarkable," Eddie agreed, sliding off the workstation and stretching to a standing position. So much had happened to this man that he didn't appear to have processed most of it.

"Hey, kid!" Hatch called to the back. "Get over here! I have someone to introduce to you!"

"I'll be there in one second," Knox said, his voice muffled like he was in some compartment.

Eddie pointed to the tires on the DeLorean, which were bald. "You're gonna have to get a new set of wheels for that car before taking her for a spin on the open roads."

Hatch glanced at the car and shook his head. "Nah. Where we're going, we don't use roads."

Julianna cast the mechanic another skeptical glance. "What exactly are you working on?"

Knox bustled out from the back carrying a tool box in both hands, grease streaked over one cheek.

"Hey, kid, I want you to meet someone special," Hatch said as Knox hustled came forward, his eyes pointed down in concentration as he lugged the heavy tools. "This is Cheng."

Knox's head jerked up and the toolboxes clattered loudly to the floor. His eyes widened and his mouth shot open. "Dad?"

Hatch's Lab, *Ricky Bobby*, Tangki System

Knox blinked, his mouth tightening with disbelief. *This wasn't possible*—and yet the brown eyes of the man who stared at him were unmistakably his father's. His feet felt stuck to the ground, and he leaned forward but didn't budge. All noise in the lab vanished, as if it had been sucked into a vacuum. He was only faintly aware that the others were staring at him with stunned expressions.

Knox's dad peered at him, shaking his head as if trying to dispel an illusion. "Dominic...Is that you?"

"'Dominic?'" Hatch asked, all his tentacles still. "Knox is your son?"

Knox was still leaning forward, but his knees gave way, making him stumble, falling hard to the ground. Julianna rushed over to help him up.

The shock of the moment took over her face, but Knox barely noticed. His focus was on the man on the other side of the room. Even from that distance, he recognized the once-familiar face. *How long had it been? Eight years?* he wondered. *No, ten.* It had been ten years since he had last seen his father.

"Gunner? No, that can't be," Hatch said, letting out a startled sigh. "He's your... No, he's my apprentice. This is Knox Gunnerson." The Londil was babbling, probably overwhelmed by the strangeness of the moment.

Knox rubbed his knee where he'd landed on one of the tools he'd dropped. His eyes were still pinned on the man standing so far away. Limping forward, Knox drew in a breath. "Is that really you...Dad?" The name seemed strange to say, making his throat tighten.

Hatch's mouth fell open, as did Julianna's and Eddie's.

It *was* him, and somehow Knox knew it. Under the shaggy black hair and beard, he recognized the man before him. A child never forgets the face of their parent. Knox could still see his mother's face swim into his vison when he closed his eyes, having memorized the photo of her taken right before she gave birth to him. That had been her last day alive, and Knox the final offering she gave to the world.

Knox' father rubbed his eyes and blinked at his son. He hadn't budged as Knox drew closer. With a shaky finger his father pointed in Knox's direction and looked at Eddie, who was beside him. "Is he real?"

Eddie, much like Hatch, appeared frozen, as if he didn't know how to react in a situation of this magnitude. "Very much so. Do you think that Knox is your son? The one who disappeared after your experiment?"

"Dominic," Knox's father corrected. "And I know he is. I'd know him anywhere."

It had been so long since Knox had heard his real name. Dominic Sung. His first name had been affectionately given to him by his mother, apparently. Knox' father had allowed it, although he'd wanted him to have a family name. Knox had abandoned both of his names when his father had disappeared, fearing that he was running for his life. And that was exactly what he had done when his father hadn't returned.

Knox remembered watching his father's paranoia grow weeks before his disappearance. He'd set booby traps in front of the entrances to their house, making up excuses that they were an experiment. He peered through the drapes at night, expecting that someone was watching them from the shadows. Maybe Knox's father didn't think he had seen this, but the young boy had been incredible at observation. He had known there was danger approaching.

The experiments... Memories flooded in, now that Knox permitted himself to remember. He recalled the experiments. The technology lying around. His father always hunched over his workstation. But at age ten, Knox hadn't known much about what his father did.

"D-D-Dad," Knox stuttered, halting a few feet away. "Where have you been?"

Knox's father shook his head and scratched his arms. "I..." he began, tears welling in his eyes. "I can't believe this. This can't be real."

It was too much to process at once, Knox agreed, but there was no mistake. The man he had thought was dead stood before him somehow. "Dad, where were you? Did you leave me?" The hurt he'd harbored for so long betrayed him, was heavy in his words.

"No!" Cheng said, appalled. "I never would do that. I made a mistake, and then...I couldn't get back to you. I'm sorry."

Now that Knox was really looking at his father, he realized how thin he was. His clothes were dirty and patched. He remembered that the man before him had always been freshly shaven, with his hair meticulously slicked back. They used to argue about Knox's...well, *Dominic*'s Mohawk. His father had disapproved of such a bold hairstyle.

"But what happened to you?" Knox asked, his arms awkwardly hanging limp by his side. He didn't know what to do with them—shouldn't they hug or something? But the man before him was a stranger, and yet he was the one person he'd longed to see for so many years. How many times had Knox wished to see his father again? He hadn't owned anything since fleeing his home, but without a doubt he would have given up everything to see his father. To know he was alive.

Instead, Knox had pushed out all thoughts connected to his father. When one lived on the streets, dwelling on the past wasn't how one survived. Knox'd had to hunt for food, and steal to meet basic his needs. Hide from bullies. There was never time to worry about his dad, but his subconscious wouldn't allow him to forget. For the last ten years his father's face had filled his sleeping dreams—filled them with the eyes that stared at him now.

"Dominic, I'm sorry!" Knox's father shook his head, seeming to fight a battle within. "I'm so sorry."

"What did you do, Dad?" Knox asked. "Why did you disappear?"

"I made a mistake, and I've been punished for it ever since."

Now that Knox was paying attention to his father's words he noticed how slow they were, not full of the vibrancy he'd had before. The look in his dad's eyes also hinted that a bit of dementia had crept into his mind. He shook when he lifted his hand, his fingers appearing to be counting all of a sudden.

"What did you do, Dad?" Knox asked.

Shame covered Cheng's face. "I forgot that you were the most important priority in my life, and I risked our lives for science."

"The people you were afraid of—did they take you?" Knox asked.

"The Saverus were watching you even then?" Eddie interjected.

Knox remembered that Eddie, Julianna, and Hatch were watching all of this—an audience to this strange reunion.

Cheng nodded. "Yes. I kn-kn-knew they were watching, and I f-f-feared they were getting close. That was one reason I wanted to finish the project and move on from it."

"Dad, you have to tell me everything. I've been in the dark all these years," Knox said. He had so many questions, and the biggest one was, how had the universe found a way to bring them back together? Knox could have ended up anywhere and his father could have come aboard any ship, but they both ended up here on *Ricky Bobby*. What were the odds?

"Dom, I'll tell you everything," Knox's father said, stepping forward to lay a hand on his son's shoulder, "but first I need a moment to appreciate that my greatest wish has come true." He pulled Knox into him and wrapped his arms around his son.

14

Officer's Lounge, *Ricky Bobby*, Tangki System

The paint on the walls hadn't even dried, but the lounge was already packed. Julianna stopped in the doorway, eyeing the neon signs that had been hung over the dart boards in the corner where some of Fletcher's team were horsing around. *Good idea...roughhouse while holding sharp objects,* she thought.

On the other side of the large area, some of the crew were using a row of pool tables. The bar itself was packed, all the stools taken.

Julianna peered down at her stalker and Harley blinked back at her, his brown eyes intently watching her every move. "We still don't have *Ricky Bobby's* cloak ready, but the bar is functioning. Priorities, right?"

"Morale is an important part of keeping a ship functioning," the ship's AI interrupted, his voice coming through the speaker in the hall next to the entryway. The noise from the bar would have drowned out his words otherwise. "Think of morale as one of the engines."

Harley turned his head to the side as if he were considering this notion.

"That's a valid point," Julianna said. She hadn't had an opportunity to talk much to Ricky Bobby since they had moved to the new ship.

"Do you have a question for me?" Ricky Bobby asked.

He had always been so perceptive. It kind of felt like he was still in her head. "Is it strange for you to have so many people around?"

"Since I have been alone for so long—is that what you mean?" Ricky Bobby asked.

"Yes," Julianna said, unsure why she felt so nervous suddenly.

"Research isn't as lonely as most would think. The work is quite stimulating," Ricky Bobby explained, not really answering the question.

"I wasn't implying that you were lonely before," Julianna stated.

"I'm not done either," Ricky Bobby said, no offense in his voice. "I was going to say that being around people in this new setup is actually lonelier for me, because it requires that I step outside myself."

Ha! Did he just say that? "Step outside himself?" Pip asked in Julianna's head.

Shush it. Adults are talking, she spat.

Meow!

"You *are* quiet on the ship," Julianna observed.

"To answer your question, I'm not used to having

others around. My research missions were solo affairs," Ricky Bobby told her.

"And you're lonelier now than before, when you actually were alone? Is that what you're saying?" Julianna asked.

Mind blown. It's like the notion, how do I feel what I'm not feeling? Pip stated.

Are you not happy unless you're interrupting?

Or how about knowing what we don't know.

Go play with Hatch, Julianna told him.

"Now that I'm not doing my research, I'm realizing that I'll have to fill the void another way," Ricky Bobby stated.

"This is your ship now," Julianna said plainly.

"Yes, and my ship should be what gives me purpose."

"But you're going to have to put yourself out there in a different way than you're used to," Julianna said.

"And you of all people know what a challenge that poses."

"I know that you're in a supreme place to be successful at such a task," Julianna said honestly. "General Reynolds picked you for this ship because he knew you were the best fit. You just need time to warm up to the crew."

"Tell me, how long did it take you? To warm up to the crew?" Ricky Bobby asked.

She knew him well enough to know that Ricky Bobby had guessed the answer to that question. "It took a while. I'm trying to be patient with myself. One day this will feel like home and the people will be family, and I think I get closer to that every day."

"But just like me, you have to *try*," Ricky Bobby said, that quiet poetic tone in his voice.

Julianna didn't reply, only nodded, then strolled into

the lounge area and over to a set of tables where Eddie and the gang were playing cards. Harley bounded around her as she walked, nearly tripping her as he darted for Marilla. He rocked back and placed his paws on her lap, enjoying the attention she gave him after the greeting.

For some reason Eddie thought that Julianna looked ruffled when she strode into the lounge. It was something about the way her shoulders were pinned up higher than usual.

Since witnessing the reunion of Knox and Cheng he'd been in observation mode. The strangeness of the surprise meeting still coursed through Eddie. It was hard for him to believe that the father and son had run into each other after a decade apart. Eddie sensed that Hatch was having a hard time processing it all, too. His research partner and his apprentice were related. What were the odds? Life was so strange.

Eddie suspected that Knox and Cheng would need much time to fill in all the gaps. They were still in Hatch's lab. Eddie and Julianna had left them to answer each other's questions and marvel that they had been reunited at all. It probably felt like a dream.

"Jules, pull up a seat," Eddie said, indicating one of the chairs at the neighboring table. He, Lars, Chester, and Marilla were gathered around a high bar table.

"What are you playing?" she asked, shoving a chair between him and Lars.

"'Cards Against Humanity,'" Chester informed her.

"Sounds like a game that is counterintuitive to Ghost Squadron's mission," she stated.

Chester scoffed at her, pushing his thick-rimmed glasses up his nose. "That's only because you haven't played it. We all need a chance to show our more morbid side. How else are we going to keep doing what we do? Fighting the good fight?"

"By knowing that it serves the greater good," Julianna said flatly. She was playing up the dry humor, which Eddie found entertaining.

"Well, and defending the Federation. Don't forget about that," Marilla stated.

Eddie dealt Julianna in from a deck of white cards. "It's a fairly easy game to play. One person picks up a black card and reads it, and there is a blank. You fill it in with one of those cards." He pointed to the white cards now in her hand.

Julianna's eyes widened as she read the cards in her hand, which said offensive things. That was the point. "What's the goal of this game?"

"The person who reads the black cards reads everyone's answer, and the most offensive or entertaining one is the winner," Chester explained.

"In essence, we're each trying to be the biggest asshole," Lars said, his tone neutral.

"Okay, well, I don't really have a soul." Julianna fanned out her cards in her hand, taking a deep breath. "Let's go for it."

Eddie picked up a black card from the center deck and read, "Instead of coal, Santa now gives the bad children *blank*."

He watched as everyone at the table shuffled through their cards to find the cleverest match. Marilla giggled, which earned her a curious look from Chester.

"And when you read the cards, you don't know whose card is whose?" Julianna asked, hesitating with the white card in her hand.

"That's right," Eddie said.

She scooted the card across the table at him.

"But of course, if I pick your card as the winner you're going to have to fess up," he said and watched as her face flushed pink.

Noise erupted at the bar as the crew cheered for one of the pilots to chug a drink.

"We should shut them down soon," Julianna said over her cards to Eddie.

"Come on, Jules—they're just getting started." He picked up the bottle of whiskey next to him and poured a shot into an empty glass, indicating with a nod that it was hers.

"Thanks," Julianna said, lowering her cards and taking a sip.

When everyone had turned in their cards, Eddie shuffled them before picking up the stack.

"Now it's time to see how demented you all are," Eddie said.

"No one can beat my wickedness," Chester stated proudly.

Julianna slammed the glass down after finishing it. Eddie winked at her and read the black card, "Instead of coal, Santa now gives the bad children..." He looked at the first white card. "Soup that is too hot."

Chester revolved in Marilla's direction, shaking his head at her. "That's your card, isn't it?"

"Chest, shhhh. It's supposed to be a secret," Marilla said, embarrassed.

"Didn't you have something crude in that stack of cards?" he asked.

"Yes, but it was all highly offensive..." Marilla's voice trailed away. She probably realized she was fairly bad at the game, and Eddie actually liked that about her. Someone on the crew had to be good at heart.

"Okay, next one," Eddie said, rereading the black card. "Instead of coal, Santa now gives the bad children..." He pulled up the next white card. "A mopey zoo lion."

Chester let out an impatient sigh. "Let me guess...Lars. That one was yours? Come on, people. Am I the only one who came to play?"

"You're not supposed to call out whose card you think it is," Marilla complained.

Chester held up his hands in surrender. "It was just a guess."

"But now we know it wasn't *your* card," Julianna stated matter-of-factly.

"Or do you? Maybe it was a ruse," Chester said slyly.

"Okay, once again," Eddie stated, picking up the next white card. "Instead of coal, Santa now gives the bad children...a lifetime of sadness." Eddie slapped the card down away from the other two answers. "Damn, that's dark and funny as hell."

Lars laughed. "Yeah, that one will be hard to beat."

Chester was having a hard time hiding his giddy glee. That answer had obviously been his.

"Last one," Eddie said, pulling up the last white card. "Instead of coal, Santa now gives the bad children…" His mouth fell open when he read the answer. "Dead parents."

Chester exploded with laughter, throwing his hand in Julianna's direction. "Damn it! I was just bested by a newbie."

Julianna released a small smile, not giving away much.

"Commander, if that is in fact your card, then you're the winner," Eddie said, sliding the card in her direction. She took it and bowed her head slightly.

"I've had a couple lifetimes to hone my skill at games like this," Julianna stated.

Eddie was halfway done dealing a new hand when Hatch waddled into the lounge. Since he was rarely seen outside his lab, he earned the attention of most in the bar. The mechanic hurried over to their table and placed a file between Julianna and Eddie, displacing a few of the cards.

"That one," Hatch said with finality, like they should all know what he was referring to.

Eddie and Julianna exchanged looks of uncertainty. "That one *what?*" Eddie asked.

"That one. That's the Chief Engineer I want," Hatch stated.

"Oh," Julianna said with surprise, picking up the file. Her eyes widened when she opened it. "But she's—"

"*That's the one I want.* Her or no one," Hatch said definitively.

Julianna nodded and laid the file back down, keeping her hand on it. "We'll discuss it with Jack. I'm sure we can make it work."

Eddie eyed the file, but decided against trying to pry it

away from Julianna. There would be time for that. This was teambuilding time, which was important to the captain. They could fight on an ongoing basis because they took time like this to bond.

"I trust you to make it happen, Julie," Hatch said, turning and waddling back the way he'd come. "Just don't let the captain screw it up."

Eddie handed Julianna a black card. "I think he secretly likes me, but admitting such a thing would destroy the incredible act we have going."

"Do you now?" Julianna asked, taking the card. "Okay, here's the question you're to answer..." She cleared her throat and read, "I drink to forget *blank?*"

Everyone around the table shuffled through their cards for the best match. *Playing Cards Against Humanity was a great way to see how everyone thought,* Eddie mused. Marilla was sensitive, and therefore picked the safe answers. Lars was respectful, and therefore chose answers that wouldn't offend. Chester, as a hacker, always tried to push the limits. And Julianna, he suspected, had a hidden wit that could best them all.

"The answers are," Julianna read the black card again, "I drink to forget..." she picked up the first card and her face dropped in irritation. "Alcoholism."

"Nice one," Eddie said with a laugh.

She picked up the next card. "I drink to forget...Harry Potter erotica."

Marilla covered her face with her hands. "That didn't just happen!"

"I assure you that it did." Chester pointed a finger at her and fired.

"I drink to forget...waking up half-naked in a Denny's parking lot."

"Been there and done that, am I right?" Eddie said to Lars, the two slapping hands.

"And the last answer is, I drink to forget..." Julianna read the final white card. "Being a motherfucking sorcerer."

Everyone at the table erupted in laughter, and it went on and on. Several times when it began to wane Eddie looked at Lars or Julianna at Chester, and as if the fuse had been relit, the laughter reignited.

"The obvious winner is 'motherfucking sorcerer,'" Julianna stated between attempts to breathe through the laughter. She held up the card, waiting for one of the men to grab it.

Marilla, whose face was still covered by her hands, pulled one away and extended it.

Chester turned to her with awe on his face. "Mar, that was you?"

"Yes, it was," she said, laying the black card in front of her as her first win.

Eddie smiled. Maybe he didn't know everything about his crew. They *could* surprise him from time to time.

"Well, I think we've proven that you are all a bunch of soulless and demented freaks," Eddie said, pushing up and away from the table. He looked down affectionately at the crew. "And I wouldn't have you any other way."

15

Jack Renfro's Office, *Ricky Bobby*, Tangki System

"Is Hatch crazy?" Eddie asked, lounging on the plush leather sofa in Jack's office.

Julianna was focused on an aquarium filled with vibrant fish. There was no doubt Felix Castile had had expensive tastes. Every inch of the office Jack had inherited from the evil mastermind reeked of his desire for finer things. The oil paintings of hunting dogs hanging on the walls and the antique vases in the corner weren't really her style, but she could get used to walking across Persian rugs and having a diffuser with essential oils running in her personal quarters.

I heard that, Pip announced in her head.

What, now I'm not allowed to like things?

I just find it amusing that you would enjoy such creature comforts.

I'm not a robot, you know? she answered.

I didn't, actually. The rumor is that there's a panel in your back where you can be turned on and off.

"What he's asking for is definitely a small wonder," Jack said, pouring bourbon into a crystal glass from a decanter and handing it to Julianna.

"I can't believe this applicant was even on the list for the chief engineer position." Eddie tapped the file that Hatch had given them the night before in the lounge. They'd brought it straight to Jack the next morning. He had, as usual, already been privy to the applicant Hatch favored. How he knew everything before them was curious.

"She actually wasn't," Jack informed them, filling his own glass. He eyed Eddie's feet, which were stretched across the long sofa. At the subtle cue Eddie dragged his feet off and sat upright, giving Jack a place to sit on the other end of the couch.

Julianna set her drink on the side table at the other end of the sofa. "Are you saying that Hatch went and dug up this applicant on his own?"

Jack nodded, leaning forward with his elbows on his knees. "This applicant didn't even surface when I was constructing the pool of potential chief engineers."

"Then how did he find her?" Julianna asked.

"I think I can shine some light on that one," Ricky Bobby stated.

"You gave him this person's information?" Eddie asked.

"Dr. A'Din Hatcherik asked me to give him the files on the previous chief engineers for this ship," Ricky Bobby said simply. "There were a total of two."

"So Hatch *is* insane." Eddie shook his head and drained

his glass. "He thinks we should employ the engineer who worked for Felix Castile. Maybe we should just invite the entire traitorous crew back."

"Actually, most of Felix's crew didn't know about his evil plans," Jack began. "He compartmentalized most of his projects, assigning bits and pieces to various personnel. I think only his closest advisors were aware of what he was really up to."

"I suspect that Dr. A'Din Hatcherik thinks that this person, Ms. Liesel Magner, would be most qualified to be the ship's engineer because of her familiarity with its inner workings," Ricky Bobby stated.

Julianna mused on the notion. "The upgrades are about bringing the ship up to Federation standards, though. How would someone who worked on a ship outside the Federation be the most qualified for that?"

"Because no one knows how to best accomplish that than the person who has cared for the ship in the past," Ricky Bobby said.

Jack rose, setting his glass on the marble end table. "The logic does make sense. I've researched Liesel, and she's actually a good applicant. Felix terminated her after she refused to make an upgrade that she deemed dangerous."

Julianna perked up at this news. "What kind of upgrade?"

Jack looked up, waiting for Ricky Bobby to interject, and on cue the AI said, "The order involved nuclear weapons. The Chief Engineer declined to implement the project."

"And Felix fired her," Eddie stated, sliding his fingers over his stubbled chin.

"Not just fired her," Jack declared. "Felix, according to my intel, had her thrown in the Brotherhood jail on Kezza."

"Because she refused to put nukes on the ship?" Julianna asked, repulsed. She was starting to like this woman.

Jack nodded. Pressing his hands together, he tilted his chin to the ceiling. "Ricky Bobby, did Hatch know about this?"

"Yes, I gave him all the details I had on Liesel Magner," Ricky Bobby stated. "I'm certain that her thorough knowledge of the ship and her unwillingness to comply with Felix Castile's request were two of the main reasons Dr. A'Din Hatcherik picked her for the position."

"The inmates of the Brotherhood jail on Kezza were all freed after we disbanded them. Liesel would be out now," Eddie stated.

Jack pressed his steepled hands to his lips before saying, "I'm afraid it's not that easy."

Eddie laughed. "Why am I not surprised?"

Jack lifted the crystal decanter and refilled his glass. "Felix, as we're all aware, held onto his grudges. Maybe he knew the Brotherhood couldn't hold Liesel for long, or he wanted to ensure that if she was freed she'd still have hardship."

"What did he do?" Julianna asked, leaning forward and narrowing her eyes.

Jack let out a sigh. "Felix, with his many connections, ruined Liesel 's reputation as an engineer. I checked her previous references, and none of them were willing to speak with me about her."

"Felix bought them out, didn't he?" Eddie asked, raising his large feet and setting them on the center ottoman.

"Or he threatened them," Julianna added.

"And we all know that without anyone to speak for your reputation it's impossible to get a credible job inside or outside the Federation," Jack stated.

Eddie chuckled. "I can't imagine this Liesel woman trying to get a job with the Federation after working for Felix."

"She did stand up to him," Julianna argued.

"Eddie's right though," Jack began. "Liesel was ruined. She wasn't going to be applying with the Federation or any other venture."

"Then what makes you think we can get her to set foot back on this ship?" Julianna asked. "This is the very place her ruin began. She probably hates it."

A sneaky grin flicked across Jack's mouth. "I have to say, transitioning from *ArchAngel* to *Ricky Bobby* has taken some getting used to. However, as a spymaster I very much appreciate working with someone who is a research expert."

Julianna observed that Jack didn't appear as quietly melancholy as he had at their last meeting. He still didn't have the same pep in his step, but a bit of the old Jack seemed to have resurfaced. "Do you mean Ricky Bobby helped you?" she asked.

Jack nodded triumphantly. "I asked him to assist me in finding anything we could use to leverage Liesel 's assistance."

"And I'm guessing that the detective didn't disappoint," Eddie spouted.

"I reviewed video logs that Liesel had recorded about ship projects," Ricky Bobby began. "I found that in all the logs, in the background or sometimes on her person, there was a ferret."

"'Ferret?' Is that like a cat?" Eddie asked.

Jack's eyes sparkled as he laughed. "Yes, I think they are similar, although I've never seen one in person."

"How is this cat-thing going to help us?" Julianna asked.

"Well, we only need to follow a single lead to find answers," the great spymaster said. He picked up a remote from his desk and clicked it once. The screen behind his desk flickered to life, and a mostly blue planet rotated in the black and star-lit space.

Julianna's gaze shifted from the screen to Jack. "What does the planet Kai have to do with this?"

"Remember Pistris Station on Kai?" Jack asked.

"How could I forget?" Eddie said with a chuckle. "That was where I stole the Stingray."

"Exactly. And with Marilla's help, I was able to track down a laboratory in Pistris Station where they hold different animals," Jack stated, the lightness on his face dropping.

"Don't tell me they do tests on them?" Julianna asked.

Jack's mouth formed a hard line and he looked at the screen where the planet Kai was still rotating. "Chester was able to hack into the laboratory's records and found that a ferret was transferred to the facility recently. The timeline matches up with Liesel 's termination."

"So Felix threw Liesel in jail and sent her pet to a Trid lab? What a fucker," Eddie seethed. "Someone should shoot him in the head."

"Ha-ha," Julianna said before returning her attention to Jack. "Are you thinking that we need to go rescue this ferret? That if we have the ferret, Liesel will be more inclined to accept the position?"

Jack clasped his hands behind his back and nodded. "That's exactly what I'm thinking. We have to earn her loyalty, because she's been burned badly."

Eddie sighed. "It seems like a convoluted way to recruit an engineer."

"I agree," Jack said at once. "But this is the applicant Hatch wants, so does one of you want to tell him you're picking someone else, or do we try and recruit her?"

Eddie and Julianna looked straight at each other, the same reluctance on both their faces.

"Convoluted plan it is," Julianna declared.

"Where's Liesel?" Eddie asked. "Have you been able to track down where she went after being discharged from the Brotherhood jail?"

A hesitant expression filled Jack's face. "Not yet. Leave that to me, though. I'll figure out where she is." He cleared his throat, looking between Eddie and Julianna. "Your job is to find the ferret."

Eddie pulled his feet off the ottoman and stood. "That is one order I never thought I'd hear you give us."

16

Stingray, Planet Kai, Tangki System

Julianna had only taken the stolen Stingray out on one other occasion. Flying the ship was different than the Black Eagles, but it hadn't been a huge learning curve. In typical fashion, Eddie and she had roshamboed for the mission since only one of them could go to Pistris Station. They had just the one Stingray, which was their only way into the underwater facility.

"As the only person on the team who has been in Pistris Station, I was the logical choice for this mission," Eddie grumbled over the comm.

"Don't sulk. It isn't attractive," Julianna retorted, steering the ship through an asteroid belt. She had to give it to the Trids. This ship had superior handling.

"So otherwise I'm a total hottie, is that what you mean?" Eddie asked, mischief in his voice.

"You're not a total dog is all I'm saying," Julianna said. There was loud barking over the comm. "Would you get that damn mutt off the bridge? We're running a ship, not a pound."

"I think he's worried about you," Eddie said, sounding amused.

"Tell him I'm bringing him a chew toy."

Another bark echoed over the comm. "I think he heard you."

"Entering Kai's atmosphere." Julianna flipped several switches overhead, following the reentry procedures for the Stingray Hatch had taught her.

"Copy that, Strong Arm," Eddie said, a strange tension in his voice.

Julianna stopped herself from making a joke about how the captain might be worried for her since she realized that everyone on the bridge was listening. Silly banter was one thing, but blurring the lines...well, that was never going to happen.

Your entry point is coming up, Pip informed her.

I see the coordinates.

Oh, so you're paying attention, then. Thought you were worrying about something else, Pip joked.

Would you get out of my head? You hear half-thoughts and think you know everything.

Give me a body to control and I'll happily get out of your head.

Liar.

You're right. I'll be here forever. Stuck to you like glue.

Eeewww!

The Stingray cruised over the shimmering blue waters of Kai and arced over the horizon where the sun was streaking the sky with pinks and oranges as it set. To the west a patch of brown land was visible, but Julianna was headed for the underwater facility under the equator.

Like the last time they had broken into Pistris Station, they were entering after-hours when the staff was lighter. Moreover, the Stingray should keep Julianna from being noticed when she entered the landing bay. Sneaking around the station would be another story, but Eddie had done it before and she could, too. Julianna still couldn't believe what she was going through for a single ferret. This Liesel must be a damn good engineer.

"I still say we buy Liesel a new ferret and pass it off as hers," Julianna stated.

Eddie chuckled. "I think she'd know."

"You don't even know the woman," Julianna argued, plunging the ship into the placid waters of Kai. Bubbles engulfed the nose of the ship, blinding Julianna momentarily. The radar told her where Pistris' landing dock was, so she knew she had time for the bubbles to clear.

"If you replaced Harley with a different dog I'd know," Eddie stated matter-of-factly. "We know our pets through and through, like we know people. They can't simply be replaced."

"Yeah, I guess you're right." Julianna squinted through the bubbles. It was such a strange thing to fly an aircraft through water. The weight of the ship had shifted considerably as it plummeted, and she felt the league of water above her now, burying the ship deeper and deeper. When she reached the second landing bay for Pistris Station, Julianna straightened out the nose and zoomed straight into the blackness.

Eddie had walked her through the process for entering the underwater facility, but still she wasn't entirely prepared for the strangeness of flying the ship through the black waters of the entry tube.

After flicking her eyes at the radar Julianna corrected before the ship grazed a wall. The landing bay was a series of zigzagging tunnels that emptied into the dry warehouse at the bottom of the facility.

Chester was currently scrambling the station's sensors, which meant their radar wouldn't pick up Julianna's arrival. However, when the ship sat dripping wet on the landing bay floor some questions might arise.

The mission was straightforward. Land. Stroll up to the top floor. Grab a ferret. Run back down. Fly away. It was a plan that relied on dutiful strategy and a hell of a lot of luck.

Dim light shone through the water ahead, and Julianna slowed the Stingray and turned in that direction. The ship plunged through the surface of the water, cruising toward the vast warehouse ahead.

To Julianna's horror, two other Stingrays were steering onto the ramp. Firstly, she had hoped that the static-filled comm they were listening to would disguise her sudden arrival. Secondly, she had prayed that the tint on the Stingray's windshield was dark enough that the Trids couldn't see her inside the ship. The bright lights did little to make her feel confident in that hope.

Taking her first opportunity to get away from the taxiing ships, Julianna steered to the back of a line of parked Stingrays.

"Status update." Eddie's voice crackled over the comm.

"The fish has landed, but the school isn't asleep," Julianna said.

"How many?" Eddie asked tightly.

"Two," Julianna whispered, watching between the ships in front of her as the first Stingray sped down and out through the launch tunnel.

"So they *are* active right now," Eddie guessed.

"It appears so," Julianna stated. The second Stingray idled behind where the first had been and she said to it, "Get the fuck out of here."

"Isn't it fun to be sitting in the belly of the whale?" Eddie asked.

"It's a rush, I'll give you that," Julianna stated.

"Strong Arm," Chester said over the comm.

"Yes, Cheshire. You got good news for me?" Julianna asked.

"All news is relative, but no," Chester said, his tone flat. He was in hacker mode. "Pip is sending me intel on the Trids' mainframe, which he's hooked into while you're in close proximity."

"And?" Julianna asked.

"It appears that for some odd reason they've upped their security measures," Chester stated.

"That *is* odd. It's like someone recently broke into their station," Eddie said with a hint of a laugh in his voice.

"What does that mean, Cheshire?" Julianna's voice was growing less patient.

"It means that although I can get you through the building, they're going to damn well know about it," Chester said quickly.

"Fuck," Eddie stammered. "Abort mission. This isn't worth it."

Julianna shook her head, although none of them could see it. She watched as the second Stingray launched. "No, I'm already here. There are two Stingrays now outside around the perimeter. Either they'll spot me, or I'll be spotted inside the facility. I'm going to take my chances."

"So, you're going to climb to the top of Pistris Station and then what? Shoot your way out?" Eddie sounded mad now. No, not mad. *Agonized.*

"Indiana Jones and I discussed Pistris based on her knowledge," Chester began, referring to Marilla's callsign. "She was advised by that Trid, Rex—the one who informed us the last time we attempted to enter the facility."

"Give me good news," Julianna said, drumming her hands on the controls.

"I might have another strategy to get you out of there, but…" Chester trailed away, a weight in his voice.

"But what?" Eddie boomed.

"But it's going to involve you rushing in for a rescue mission, captain," Chester said, an edge of reluctance in his voice.

"Why didn't you say so?" Eddie retorted. "Fuck, yeah! I'll suit up now."

"Wait, rescue mission? I'm no fucking damsel in distress," Julianna argued.

"No, you definitely aren't," Eddie said, his tone different now…thoughtful. "You're part of a team, and sometimes we have to rely on each other."

"Strong Arm, this is the only way if you want to complete the mission," Chester told her. "You can get up there, but there's little hope of you getting back down. If you want to get out of Pistris Station, someone will have to pick you up."

"While I'm holding a fucking ferret, need I remind you?" Julianna almost laughed at the absurdity of this all. "And yeah, fine. Get your ass out this way, Blackbeard, but stay cloaked. There are two Stingrays cruising around."

"Copy that, Strong Arm," Eddie stated. "Stay in communication."

"Blackbeard, I'm sending over the coordinates for the rendezvous," Chester said.

"Thanks, Cheshire," Eddie said. "I hope this plan of yours works."

"There's a probability of seventy-four percent that it will," Ricky Bobby chimed over the comm.

"It's that twenty-six percent chance that bothers me," Eddie said.

Eddie sped the Q-Ship out of the bay, with Lars in the copilot's seat. He wanted to slam his fist into something, but how could he be mad at Julianna for making exactly the same decision he would have made? Of course she wasn't going to abandon a mission when she was already on the premises, and then Chester had given them a backup plan. He definitely would have carried out the mission then—but something about this all made his insides fester.

He kept reminding himself that Julianna was different. She was enhanced. Unlike so many Eddie had lost Julianna couldn't be easily defeated, but for that very reason it was more difficult. Julianna *was* different. Losing her would be...*worse.*

"Enemy ships approaching portside," Lars informed him as they barreled over the waters of Kai.

This was a stealth mission, so they couldn't engage. Eddie banked hard to starboard, keeping as much distance between them and the Stingrays as possible.

The Kezzin had at one point been able to spot the Q-Ships with heatseeking technology even when cloaked, but Hatch had figured out ways to confuse their systems. Hopefully it wouldn't be a problem here, since Eddie needed to be in place and ready. The last thing he needed was to fight a couple of Stingrays and make Julianna wait.

"Another enemy ship advancing," Lars stated, pointing his long scaly finger at the radar.

"Damn it!" Eddie sputtered, igniting the thrusters and lifting the Q-Ship away from the surface of the water where Julianna would soon be waiting. It was too dangerous to be that low with the Stingrays making rounds.

"Strong Arm," Eddie whispered over the comm. "What's your status?"

Julianna pressed her back to the wall as the door to the stairwell nearly smacked into her face. She'd heard the Trids approaching just before the door swung open, so with no other option Julianna had slid behind it. It would block her from view as the Trid soldiers filed down the stairs and through the door. Grabbing the handle to keep it close, Julianna used the door to shield herself until the Trids had started down the next set of stairs.

"Strong Arm!" Eddie bellowed over the comm. "Do you copy?"

"Yes," she whispered, her voice barely audible. What the hell? Did Eddie want her to get caught responding to him?

"Fuck! I thought something happened to you," he said breathlessly.

Julianna let the door go and took a breath before rushing up the stairwell, continuing her trek to the top. Having a personalized cloak would have been ideal, but Hatch had said that the belts had to be reworked to utilize the aether crystals they'd brought back from Berosia.

"Cheshire, are you intentionally keeping me in suspense about this secret exit strategy?" Eddie asked, his tone dripping with frustration.

A *click-clack* sound filled the comm as Chester rejoined the conversation. "I'm working on it right now. It involves overhauling their—"

"You're working on it," Julianna whispered. "That's all that matters. No details."

"It would be relevant for you to know that I'm tricking Pistris Station into thinking there's a major water leak," Chester stated.

"Why does that matter?" Julianna dared ask.

"Because it's going to trigger their alarm systems," Chester said.

"Why does that matter?" Julianna repeated, clearing the last set of stairs to the top level. "You said they were already going to know I'm here."

"Exactly, so it's worth the risk," Chester stated.

"But the alarms haven't been activated yet," Julianna replied, a bit of hope lightening her breathing. "Maybe they won't suspect I'm here."

"You're in the stairwell, right?" Chester asked.

Julianna's hand rested on the door to the corridor. "Correct."

"They're going to know as soon as you leave it," Chester said, a morose quality to his tone.

Julianna tightened her grip on the handle and pressed her ear flat to the door.

"I can't block their surveillance on such short notice," Chester continued, "not with their new upgrades. The best I can do is trick their monitoring system into thinking that the facility is being flooded."

"I'm not sure I understand," Eddie stated.

"According to Indiana Jones, the research lab is located on the top level because they employ a handful of humans," Chester began. "And because humans tend to drown in floods, there's a special exit strategy for them."

"Which is how you plan to get Strong Arm out of there," Eddie exclaimed. "Good work, Cheshire."

"Okay, it's go-time," Julianna stated, her hand tightening even more on the handle. She took a deep breath and whipped the door open.

Pistris Station, Planet Kai, Tangki System

Julianna quickly scanned the long metal corridor. The floors were an iridescent blue and the lights dim, and to her relief the space was empty. She bounded forward, sprinting for the other side. The lab where the animals were held was supposedly on the far side in the northwest corner.

The lights overhead brightened suddenly, then strobed red. A blaring alarm joined the light show.

"Fuck, I think they know you're there," Eddie said, obviously having heard the alarm over the comm.

Infrared scanners are showing approaching Trids in the intersecting corridor ahead.

The hallways did "T" ahead, but Julianna needed to follow the corridor until it dead-ended.

Where? Julianna asked, moving so fast her feet barely touched the slick floor. Maybe she could outrun them and barricade the door once she got into the lab.

When you are at the intersection, the Trids will be at your three o'clock and roughly fifteen feet away.

I can outrun that, Julianna thought.

And the others will be at your nine o'clock at approximately ten feet away.

Fuck. They're going to shoot me in the back.

Not if you take them out first, Pip offered.

All right, challenge accepted.

As Julianna ran she crossed her arms behind her back, reaching for the holstered weapons on both sides. Not jostled from the movement, she withdrew the guns. Releasing the safeties with ease, Julianna halted in the center of the intersection with her arms extended. She aimed the weapons in opposite directions down the connecting hallway and fired each gun once, knocking out her targets on each side.

The Trids fell back, but from both sides of the hallway more armed Trids rushed in Julianna's direction. With her arms still extended she fired again, but this time the sharks dodged her bullets. She dropped to one knee, firing the weapon in her right hand low and the one in her left behind her back. The next wave of Trids fell, blocking the others. A continuous swarm of Trids poured out of both ends of the hallway.

You better get out of there, Pip said in an urgent voice.

Copy that, Julianna said, springing up and sprinting toward the lab.

"Almost to the lab," Julianna said over the comm.

"I'll have it open for you in ten seconds," Chester stated.

"Don't you think you could have opened it before now?" Eddie said, sounding irritable.

"I didn't want to direct the Trids' attention to where we were headed," Chester said. "I'm sure the labs where they keep the rats was the last place they expected us to raid."

Julianna stopped in front of the door at the end of the corridor. The security light beside it still glowed red. She turned, holding up one pistol and firing off a round.

The light turned green and Julianna rushed through the door, keeping up her cover fire as she did, then pushed the door shut and heard it latch.

"I can hold them out of the laboratory for roughly ninety seconds," Chester stated.

"Is that enough time to get Strong Arm out of there?" Eddie asked.

"No, but it's enough time to get her to the safe room at the top," Chester said.

The lab was unsurprisingly filled with equipment and computer stations and from the far side, reflective eyes stared at her. Julianna rushed over to the cages. Rats, rabbits, and a strange cat-like thing were behind the bars, most of them shivering with fright. They all stared at her with fearful eyes, their little noses sniffing.

What had the Trids done to these animals—or what were they going to do to them? How could they hold them in cages like this?

"Strong Arm," Eddie said, his voice husky. "Did you locate the ferret?"

"Uhhhh...yeah." Julianna rotated, scanning for more options.

"What do you mean, 'uhhhh?'" Eddie asked, his tone clipped.

"Nothing. Just trying to figure out how to get the animal out of the cage," Julianna lied.

A loud bang assaulted the door. The Trids fired again and again at the lock, but thankfully their technology was good enough to keep them out of their own lab.

"You have roughly sixty-five seconds to get to the ladder on the far side of the room," Chester informed her. "They're trying to get around my hack, and I can't hold them out much longer."

Julianna spied a duffle bag by a workstation. She picked it up and emptied it of books and papers.

"Do you see the evacuation ladder by the entrance where you came in?" Chester asked.

Julianna opened the first cage, swiveling her head over her shoulder and barely noticing what Chester was talking about. "Yeah, got it."

"You need to be up that ladder and through the hatch in forty-five seconds," Chester stated.

Julianna opened another cage, reaching for its contents. "Ouch."

"What happened?" Eddie asked.

"Fucker bit me," Julianna stammered.

"Oh, well, the ferret is probably scared," Eddie stated.

It wasn't the ferret, but Julianna wasn't going to tell Eddie that.

"Once you're through the hatch, I can remotely seal it and activate flood mode," Chester continued as Julianna opened and cleared out each of the cages. "The compartment will detach on my signal and rise to the surface of the water, where Blackbeard will be ready."

"You're running out of time," Eddie yelled. "Are you almost done?"

Julianna opened the last cage, eyeing the tan and white ferret. He rushed for her hand, seeming to understand the urgency of the moment. She stuffed the ferret as gently as she could into the duffle bag with the other animals and ran for the ladder. With the bag across her shoulder, Julianna climbed the ladder. The Trids rushed through the now-open door.

Julianna pulled a single red ball from her pocket, and in a swift movement, she unscrewed it a half an inch and threw it behind her. A moment later a loud explosion rocked the room, nearly knocking Julianna off the ladder. She'd known she was too close to the door to use the grenade, but she'd had to try. Heat blasted her face and the explosion rang sharply in her ears, but she continued up the ladder.

Using both hands, she unscrewed the hatch. Trids were starting to stir below her, stepping over the fallen to get to her. The hatch finally released and Julianna launched herself through.

A Trid had made it to the ladder and was climbing quickly. He dove for her leg, grazing it as she made it all the way through to the other side. His teeth snapped at her as he climbed higher, but Julianna stomped down hard on the Trid's face, knocking him away.

Julianna slammed the hatch shut and rotated it closed, then threw the manual lock into place.

"I'm through," she whispered, looking around at the small pod she'd entered. It was a fifteen-by-fifteen-foot space lined with lifejackets and survival supplies. Another ladder like the one she'd just used was in front of her, and at its top was another hatch. So that was how she was getting out of here—clever thinking on Chester's and Marilla's parts.

"Oh shit! Pod detachment delayed," Chester told her urgently.

18

Pistris Station, Planet Kai, Tangki System

"What the fuck?" Eddie yelled. "What's going on?"

The pod shook violently when something exploded against the hatch at Julianna's feet. The Trids were giving it all they had.

"I'm momentarily locked out of Pistris Station," Chester said, sounding distracted. The *click-clack* from his side of the comm was a cacophony.

"How is that possible?" Eddie stated.

"They found me out," Chester explained, his voice overwhelmed with nervous frustration. "I'm trying to find a backdoor. Give me a sec."

Eddie grunted his disapproval.

Julianna circled, trying to calm the squirming animals in the duffle bag. They scurried around, many of them trying to poke their heads through the opening. She was pushing them back down when she noticed a box on the wall.

She rushed to it and said, "Wouldn't there be a way to manually deploy the pod in case of an actual flood?"

"Hmmm..." Chester mused. "I'd expect so. I would also think the Trids could override it."

"Well, there's only one way to find out." Julianna ripped open the box. A single button sat under a clear cover, below which was a lever. This seemed easy enough.

"Here goes everything," Julianna said, slamming her hand on the red button and pulling the lever down, where it locked into place.

The pod creaked, and gears groaned. Julianna lost her footing when the pod shifted.

"What's happening?' Eddie asked.

"I'm not sure," Julianna said honestly. "It's moving. I think."

The pod has disengaged, Pip informed Julianna.

"The pod is free," Julianna said, excitement pounding in her chest.

"Yeah, but the propellers need to activate to push you to the surface," Chester said, continuing to type loudly.

"Or what?" Eddie asked.

"Or else she's going to float around aimlessly," Chester stated.

"And the Trids will be on me in no time," Julianna said, her eyes running over the box where she'd activated the detachment.

"And I can't help now, since you're no longer connected to the station." Chester sounded defeated, but he wasn't the one in a cramped pod floating through the ocean with a bunch of rodents.

"The red button..." Julianna said mostly to herself. "Was that to detach?"

"Yes, Indiana Jones says that sounds right," Chester affirmed. "She also says there's a lever under that to activate the propellers. The pods are naturally buoyant, but you're pretty low and will run out of air unless you reach the surface soonish."

"You're just full of bad news today," Eddie seethed.

Julianna gritted her teeth and pulled the lever back into its starting position, then forced it back down—but nothing happened. She tried it again, with no result, and was about to kick the pod's wall when an engine hummed underneath her and the floor vibrated.

Julianna swayed to the side as the pod floated upward.

"I did it!" she yelled triumphantly. "Propellers are working. I'm headed for the surface."

"Fuck yeah!" Eddie hollered. "I'm keeping an eye out for you, Strong Arm. I'll let you know when to open the hatch."

Julianna climbed to the top of the ladder, her hands ready to spin the hatch open.

"Just so you know," Eddie began, "we have company. The Stingrays won't see you before I do, but you'd better be ready to jump onto the wing of the ship. You and that furry little ferret. I don't think we should engage if we can help it, since this is a rescue mission."

Julianna patted the bag behind her. "I agree, and don't worry—we'll be ready."

The pod rocked hard, nearly knocking Julianna off the ladder. She held on, tightening her core to stabilize herself.

"I see the top of the pod, Strong Arm! You've surfaced," Eddie said, his voice as happy as she'd ever heard it.

"I'm coming out," Julianna said, turning the hatch. After several rotations it disengaged and opened, and the night air spilled in. Julianna climbed out as the Q-Ship swooped down in front of her, momentarily uncloaked so she could find her way to the wing. Eddie hung out of the hatch with an arm extended.

Julianna sprang off the floating pod and reached for Eddie's extended hand, and she was momentarily suspended in air with her feet kicking. The ship dipped and moved closer to her, but the jump seemed to take forever. Her hands reached and reached, finding only air... and then they brushed the metal of the ship. Eddie caught her around the waist and pulled her aboard and Julianna staggered inside, careful to protect her cargo. She turned, breathless, and from the open hatch she looked down at the floating pod receding into the distance.

Lars recloaked the ship as the Stingrays caught sight of them and fired.

"Hold on tight," Lars said at the controls. "I'm going to give those ugly Trids the slip."

19

Landing Bay, *Ricky Bobby*, Tangki System

"You risked your life for rats?" Eddie yelled when Julianna finally opened the duffle bag. They'd been too distracted avoiding the Stingrays for him to notice the large duffle bag. Lars had flown brilliantly, darting around all the Trids' attacks, and once the Stingrays had lost track of the Q-Ship it was a smooth trip.

Eddie had pressed back into his seat for the rest of the flight, apparently needing time to catch his breath. Too consumed with quelling his anxiety, he hadn't even noticed Julianna stash the moving duffle bag under the seats.

Once they'd disembarked from the Q-Ship, Julianna finally checked that she hadn't unknowingly crushed a bunny or broken a rat's neck.

"I couldn't just leave them there," Julianna explained, bending down. She pulled a solid gray bunny from the bag and he sniffed her, then clawed her arm with his back feet.

She set the ungrateful rodent down and he hopped off a few paces with his nose twitching.

Lars watched wide-eyed as she pulled a rat from the bag. She was about to drop it on the landing bay floor as well, but thought better of it. Extending her hand to Lars, she said, "Can you take this one? If we have a rat infestation aboard the ship, Ricky Bobby is going to be pissed."

"'Pissed' is not the right word for it," Ricky Bobby stated. "Incredibly annoyed would be a better description."

Eddie's face was a magenta shade that Julianna had never seen him wear. "Did you even *get* the ferret?"

Julianna pushed a few mice around in the bag. They seemed content to stay in the warm enclosed space. Finally, on the side of another bunny—this one white with red eyes—Julianna found the long ferret. He had big brown eyes and a long tail, and wore a curious expression on his face.

She held up the ferret triumphantly. "I did. See?"

Eddie softened slightly, but still appeared to be somewhat upset. Marilla and Chester rushed forward—thankfully they'd left Harley behind.

Marilla halted momentarily and then rushed over and scooped up the gray bunny, cuddling it to her face. "You got a bunny?"

Eddie glared down at Julianna. "Yes, and the Commander nearly died to save that fucking pellet-dropper."

Julianna laughed. The bunny had already managed to leave behind a trail of little round poops.

"I don't see what the big deal is," Julianna said, handing

the ferret to Chester, who took it a bit reluctantly. "I got the ferret. I'm safe. Everything worked out."

"The big deal is that you keep risking your damn life to save four-legged creatures!" Eddie said so loudly that everyone's jovial expressions dropped. "You don't even like the damn things, yet you're willing to die to protect them. I don't get it."

Julianna straightened, taking a breath to steady herself. "I don't have to like something to value its life. It's why we do what do, isn't it? Because our job is to protect, no matter how large or how small that life is. If I had left these animals in Pistris Station to be used in tests and abused I wouldn't really be doing my job, would I, captain?"

Eddie's sharp eyes studied Julianna's face, which was full of conviction. "You have to pick your battles, and this seemed like a foolish risk. We signed on to protect the Federation, not a bunch of rodents."

"Wrong," Julianna countered. "We signed on to protect everything the Federation values, and that includes all life —alien, human, and animal."

Lars, Marilla, and Chester all looked at Eddie, waiting for his response to this.

He apparently didn't have one, because he shook his head. "Damn it, Jules, I don't understand you at all." He paused, and a slight smile lit up his face as he eyed the little creatures squirming in the other three's hands. The captain looked at Julianna. "However, I respect the hell out of you."

20

Jack Renfro's Office, *Ricky Bobby*, Tangki System

Jack laughed when he heard Julianna's tale of the mission at Pistris Station, with many interjections from Eddie.

"She got onto me about Harley, saying she didn't want the ship to become a pound," Eddie began, eyeing Julianna. "Then she goes off and makes it a fucking pet shop."

Jack chuckled again. "Well, we are going to have to find something to do with the animals. Maybe set them free in the woods somewhere."

"But we got the ferret, and he's safe," Julianna stated.

She is fucking unbelievable, Eddie thought with an agitation that was increasingly making him crazy. When she had been on Pistris Station he had thought Julianna was fighting Trids or having trouble locating the ferret. Little did he know that she had been clearing out all the damn cages, and yet she did it. She had fought Trids, saved a dozen animals, and figured out a way to get the pod to the surface and escape. If he'd thought she'd allow him to compliment her on the mission he would have, but right now the most he chanced was showing his respect as well as his unending irritation.

"I believe the ferret is key," Jack stated, pulling a piece of paper from his desk.

"What's with you and paper reports?" Eddie motioned to the filing cabinet Jack had moved over from *ArchAngel*.

Jack looked at the metal filing cabinet, which appeared out of place next to the high-end furnishings of Felix's old office, and shrugged. "I don't know. I've just always enjoyed holding paper. I almost feel as though I can understand the words better that way. I also only read paperback novels."

"Which as of an hour ago were delivered to your private quarters," Ricky Bobby informed them.

Jack paused, looking up as if waiting for more. When Ricky Bobby didn't say anything else Jack said, "Thank you. I missed my books."

Julianna smiled at him sideways. She'd had a different energy since returning from the mission—it must have energized a rare rebellious streak. "Were you waiting for Ricky Bobby to tell you that you should organize the titles in order to find them more efficiently?"

Jack gave Julianna an incredulous look. "Ricky Bobby, as I have learned, isn't ArchAngel."

"And that's a good thing?" Eddie asked, drawing out the last word.

"Or do you miss her incessant nagging?" Julianna wondered.

"Would you two stop? Ricky Bobby and I are very

compatible," Jack said, waving the paper. "For example, based on Liesel Magner's release date from the Brotherhood jail, we've run different scenarios that detail where she might have ended up."

"This sounds like science," Eddie said, giving Julianna a playful look.

"It's computer simulation," Ricky Bobby informed them. "All known factors were entered into the model, such as available transportation on the day of discharge, travel options, known job openings, personality information that I logged based on Liesel Magner's video records, and lodging options."

"Wow," Eddie said, meaning it. "That sounds complicated."

Jack pressed back into his seat and pointed up at the ceiling. "See, he's perfect for me! Simulations to determine likely outcomes—it's genius."

"I don't know," Julianna said, a skeptical edge in her voice. "I think you need someone to keep you in line. I could tell you how you can improve, although I do admit that Ricky Bobby is a nice compliment to your work style."

Jack shook this off with a wave of his hand. "Anyway, based on what we found, we were able to narrow down where Liesel could be to three different places. I did some digging, and the simulation proved invaluable."

"You found Liesel? Damn, that *is* impressive," Eddie said.

Jack nodded. "She's working in a bar not far from the Brotherhood jail."

"So she didn't make it off-planet," Julianna stated.

"How could she?" Jack asked. "She was penniless, her

reputation was ruined, and her emotional and mental state were most likely shattered."

"And the simulation helped you two to select this bar job as an option?" Eddie asked.

Jack nodded. "Ricky Bobby found a video log where Liesel was trying to program a robot to mix drinks."

"We therefore deduced that in her predicament she'd rely on service experience to obtain work," Ricky Bobby stated.

"Yes, it appeared from the video log that Liesel had a thorough knowledge of mixology and was trying to manually program it into the droid," Jack informed them. "I checked, and have confirmed that she does in fact work at this bar."

"Mixology knowledge! Damn it, this engineer is perfect for the ship." Eddie stood and looked down at Julianna. "Let's go recruit this woman and get a drink."

Julianna stood up. "I guess I do deserve a drink."

21

McClain's Tavern, BFE/Desert District, Planet Kezza, Tangki System

"Do you know anything about this place?" Eddie asked Lars as they strolled through the greasy doors of the bar.

Lars halted and gave Eddie a long look of contempt. "I'm from Kezza, but that doesn't mean I've been to every establishment on the planet. It's fairly large, you know."

Julianna scanned the smoky bar, pushing the ferret back into the inside pocket of her jacket. It squirmed, daring to rub its wet nose against her finger, and she withdrew her hand with disgust. Eddie had refused to carry the ferret, saying he was allergic. She was pretty sure he was still pissed about the rodent rescue mission. Lars had offered to carry the animal, but he had been salivating at the time so Julianna had declined the offer, not wanting to tempt the carnivore.

"That sounds like an excuse, Lars," Eddie said, striding into the bar, which was mostly empty. "I've frequented a ton of bars on rather large planets. What did you spend your time on Kezza doing, anyway?"

Lars followed. "Learning, working, hiking... You know, I actually didn't drink until I met up with you two."

Eddie gave Julianna a look of horror. "I believe your friend is implying we drove him to drink."

Julianna offered Lars a commiserate expression. "It's true. I've done it to the very best. It's my sullen mood. I turn people into alcoholics." She nodded in Eddie's direction. "And he's just a bad influence, plain and simple."

"I resemble that remark," Eddie said, a look of mock offense on his face.

"I'm buying you a dictionary for your birthday," Julianna said, cutting around the two men and sidling up to the dusty bar.

"I was joking. 'Resemble.' 'Resent.' It was supposed... Oh, never mind." Eddie joined her with a roguish smile on his face. "What *are* you getting me for my birthday? It's coming up, you know."

"I didn't, actually."

Julianna held up her hand to get the attention of the bartender at the far end of the counter. She was human, with light mocha skin and a tough expression that Julianna could respect. The woman wore ripped jeans and a black leather jacket. There was no doubt that this woman—their Liesel Magner—was tough, and for good reason. This place was filled with the lowest of the low.

Kezzin hooligans played cards in the corner, and there was a knife stuck into the table. In a neighboring booth, two aliens sat hunched with hoods hiding their faces. In the shadows of the darkened bar were other scoundrels, drinking their warm beers.

The woman didn't offer them a smile as she trotted over, wiping a mug with a dirty bar rag. "What can I do for you?" the woman asked in a no-nonsense tone.

"We were actually looking—"

"Look around this place," the bartender interrupted Julianna. "I don't answer questions like what you're about to ask. It doesn't matter if I've seen the Kezzin you're looking for. I'm not going to tell you anything. It's better that way."

"Actually, it's you—"

The bartender held up her hand to stop Julianna and turned to the woman who had materialized with a tray with empty glasses. In contrast to the insolent expression the bartender wore, the waitress had kind eyes. Also unlike the bartender, the waitress wore flowing bohemian pants decorated in yellows, blues, and pinks, and a knit top to match. She had short wispy blonde hair and curious blue eyes.

"Gin wants another round," the waitress said, tossing her head in the direction of the table where the Kezzin were playing cards.

Julianna watched with interest, as did Eddie and Lars.

The bartender stuck her hands on her hips. "Tell Gin that he pays in advance. I'm not letting his gang guzzle drinks they can't afford. I learned my lesson the last time, and the time before that. Good-for-nothing thieves!"

"All righty," the waitress chirped. The bangles on her wrist clanged as she trotted off.

Julianna kept an eye on the girl, worried that she was

about to walk into a bar fight. She was of average height, but lean in build. Against a gang of Kezzin, the human didn't stand a chance. The group in the back hollered loudly now, one of the Kezzin toppling his chair as he bolted upright.

"Look," Eddie began, "we're looking for Liesel Magner. Are you her?"

The bartender narrowed her green eyes at them sharply. "Who wants to know?"

"We know about Felix Castile," Julianna said. "We know what he did to you."

"You don't know anything," the bartender spat. This was going to be harder than they had thought, even though they had the ferret.

Eddie pulled out cash from his pocket and slid it across the bar. "We'll take three beers, and you can keep the change."

The bartender eyed the money. She probably never got tips here. But if she'd open up and talk to them, she wouldn't have to work at this shitty-ass bar anymore.

A bit reluctantly, she took the money and filled three dirty mugs from the tap.

Julianna merely eyed the drink when it was set in front of her. "What if we told you that we have something that you'd want? Something Felix took from you?"

The woman, who had been watching the ruckus in the back, drew her gaze to Julianna. "My dignity? My freedom? My reputation? What exactly do you have that that man took?"

Julianna started to pull the squirming ferret from her pocket when a loud crash resounded.

"Those fuckers! They break my shit and then turn tail and run," Liesel said, darting around the bar and hurrying for the back.

Lars, who had also not touched his drink, looked at Eddie and Julianna. "We don't have tails, so I resent that description."

"She's one tough cookie," Eddie said, taking a long sip of his beer. He apparently didn't have the same reservations about the drink.

The waitress hurried over to the bar carrying a tray of broken glasses. In the back, Liesel could be heard making a series of threats to the gang of Kezzin miscreants.

The waitress laughed to herself as she slid the broken glasses into the trash.

"What's so funny?" Julianna asked.

The woman looked up at the group like she hadn't noticed them before. She had a dreamy look about her. "Oh, this group does this every week, and it's always the same story. You'd think that Logan wouldn't allow them in here."

"Logan?" Eddie asked.

"Logan is the owner of the bar," the waitress said. The waitress was serenely attractive. She had old-soul eyes and an unflustered expression on her face, even with the chaos in the back.

"But the bar's name is 'McClain's,'" Lars stated.

The waitress nodded. "None of us go by our real names anymore." Her eyes slid to the side, as if she had been accosted by a sudden thought. "Maybe we've outgrown them, or they don't work for who we've had to become."

Julianna didn't really understand hippie types, but this

woman seemed to be wise and also exceptionally positive. The slight pirate smile hadn't dropped from her mouth while she talked.

The bartender made another threat—this one with a firm finality to it—then stomped back to the bar. When she was behind the counter again she roared, "I mean it, Gin! No more fighting!"

Liesel had some lungs, Julianna thought, her ears ringing. The ferret had jumped inside her jacket from the loud noise and was now clawing at her boob. *Damn it, stop it.*

"Did he pay up?" the waitress asked.

Liesel nodded. "Yeah. You can give his group another round, but then we're cutting him off."

"Okey-dokey," the waitress said, filling a row of dirty mugs.

Eddie finished his drink and slid his glass forward.

"Is that your way of asking for another?" the bartender asked.

"No, I think I'm good," Eddie said. "But back to what we were talking about before. We've sought you out because we need an engineer."

"Then why are you looking for me?" the woman asked.

"We're a rogue squadron with the Federation," Eddie began. "We got rid of Felix and took over his ship. We want the original chief engineer who—"

Liesel strode forward and slammed her hand on the bar in front of Eddie. Behind her, the waitress watched with cautious eyes. "Look, pal, I don't care about that fucking ship. Whatever problems you inherited when you took it over aren't mine."

"We figured you'd say that," Eddie said, his voice steady. "That's why—"

"Did you now?" Liesel asked with contempt in her voice. "What made you figure that out? Was it that Felix had me thrown in jail? Ruined my reputation? Stole everything I had?" She leaned in close to Eddie, her eyes hot. "Why don't you take your fucking ship and get as far away from here as possible. I want nothing to do with it."

Julianna reached into her jacket pocket, unnoticed by the bartender. "Even if I went to all the trouble and risked my life to return this guy to you?" She withdrew the ferret from her jacket and held him up above the bar.

The bartender blinked dully at Julianna, as if trying to compute what she was seeing.

It was the waitress who showed a reaction, slapping her hand to her mouth. "Sebastian!"

The ferret scratched Julianna's hand, leaving red marks. She dropped him onto the bar and he ran past Lars and Eddie, rounding the corner and then leaping off its surface. The waitress caught him in her arms, and he snuggled into her neck.

22

McClain's Bar and Grill, Warehouse District, Planet Kezza, Tangki System

"You're Liesel?" Eddie asked, staring at the hippie waitress whose ferret was trying to put his face in hers.

She giggled, tickled by the creature's whiskers. She didn't hear Eddie as she petted the ferret with tears starting to well in her eyes. The waitress lifted the ferret into the air and looked him over. "Sebastian, is this really you?" She laughed. "It has to be."

The bartender turned to Liesel. "Is that the rat you're always going on about?"

Liesel covered the ferret's ears. "He's a ferret, and doesn't like to be called a rat. That's what *that* man called him."

"Do you mean Felix Castile?" Lars said, speaking up for the first time.

Both women spun around and looked at the three. The bartender stepped forward to block the waitress, threading her arms in front of her chest. "Look, Liesel doesn't want any trouble, so why don't you all get out of here?"

"Which is why you pretended to be her," Julianna stated. "You're Logan, aren't you?"

Liesel patted the larger woman on the side of the arm. "Thanks, Logan, but I'd like to talk to these people. They did bring me Sebastian."

Logan eyed Liesel suspiciously. "You're too trusting. They obviously brought him because they want something."

Liesel laughed, her eyes brimming with merriment. "You're the one who lets Gin in here even though you know what he'll do. I know nothing about these people except that they've brought me back my best friend."

Logan seemed to consider this for a long moment and then picked up the tray. "Speaking of Gin, I'll take him the drinks before he breaks another chair. You can go on break."

"Thanks," Liesel said, setting the ferret on the counter-top. She reached underneath and pulled up a can that rattled with metal objects.

The ferret rose onto his hind legs with his little hands extended.

"Look what I have for you, Bastian," she said, rattling the can. "It's your favorite. I've been collecting them for months."

The ferret climbed up and dunked his head into the rusty can before withdrawing a sparkplug. Eddie hadn't noticed how flexible the animal was, or his remarkable dexterity.

Liesel took the sparkplug from the ferret and eyed it.

"Yep, you're right. That one is probably still good, but we'll have to test it. I think you've still got it." Her eyes were dazzled, and she was obviously overjoyed by having her pet back safely.

"Got what?" Julianna asked, her eyes glued on the strange scene before them.

"Oh, right," Liesel said, turning to the group as the ferret continued to scavenge in the can of sparkplugs. "Sebastian isn't just my best friend. He also is my assistant. He has an incredible instinct." She pointed to the can. "Those are all old sparkplugs I've found. I'm pretty certain he can still pick out the duds from the useable ones."

"No way," Lars said, his eyes wide.

"Way." Liesel turned to the ferret, who had pulled out two more sparkplugs and laid them to the side.

"Those are the usable ones?" Julianna asked, pointing to the pile starting to accumulate.

Liesel shrugged. "Probably. I've never known exactly how his mind works. He is a ferret, after all."

"Right..." Eddie said, drawing out the word. "A ferret who assisted you with ship repairs, is that right?"

"Oh, where are my manners?" Liesel said, clapping her hands together. She bowed slightly to them. "Thank you endlessly for returning Sebastian to me. I can't express how happy this makes me. I never thought I'd see him again, and now..." She clapped again, the smile never leaving her face. "I must know, how did you find Bastian?"

"This one risked my beating heart to accomplish the task," Eddie stated, pointing at Julianna.

Waving him off, Julianna said, "I had to break into a

Trid underwater base. It's done, and now you have your animal."

Liesel smiled, looking genuinely happy. "Yes, and again thank you. Now the question is why? Why did you return Sebastian to me?"

"Well, Logan is right that we want something," Julianna began, pushing her untouched beer out from in front of her.

"Oh, don't drink that. We never wash those glasses." Liesel grabbed Julianna's and Lars' mug, but paused when she looked at Eddie's empty glass, offering him an apologetic smile.

He waved her off. "Don't worry, I've drunk worse and paid more for it, both in money and aftereffects."

Liesel grabbed three new mugs from under the bar, these clear and clean. She filled and set them in front of the group.

"Thanks." Eddie lifted the mug and look a long drink. The head of the beer stuck to his lip when he pulled it away.

Julianna took a sip as well, enjoying the crispness of the beer. It wasn't half bad, considering what a dump this was. "Liesel, the reason that we're here—and brought you Sebastian—is that we have a mechanic aboard the ship you once knew as *Unsurpassed*."

For the first time, the light expression dropped from Liesel's face. "That ship only brought me problems. It was the beginning of the end for me."

"We understand that," Julianna told her, "but it doesn't have to be that way. Felix made a lot of problems for a lot of people, and we've been trying to fix them—clean up what he did."

"Then what are you doing with his ship?" Liesel asked.

It was hard for Eddie to fathom that the woman before them was the prized engineer Hatch wanted. She seemed too flowery to be a mechanic, but this just proved that appearances could in fact be deceiving.

"After we defeated Felix, we took possession of his ship," Julianna explained.

"How do I know that you're not as evil as he was?" Liesel asked. "Pirates take ships that don't belong to them."

"We defeated him, and we needed a ship. There was no reason to let a good ship go to waste," Julianna said. "And now we need your help with that ship."

"Help? With that ship?" She shook her head. "I don't know you, and I've learned my lesson about working for people I don't know."

"That's an excellent point," Eddie stated after taking another sip. "We knew you'd be unwilling to work on the ship, which is why we risked a lot to bring you Sebastian. And we also know that Felix ruined your reputation, which is why we're offering you the position of Chief Engineer aboard *Ricky Bobby*."

"My old job?" Liesel regarded him sideways, not looking at all convinced.

"Our mechanic, Dr. A'Din Hatcherik, asked for you personally for this position," Julianna explained.

"Dr. A'Din Hatcherik!" Liesel exclaimed, looking at the ferret as if checking to see if he found this ridiculous as well. "That's who your mechanic is? You really *are* with the Federation, aren't you?"

Eddie nodded his head and then lowered his voice. "Yes and no. We work on missions on the frontier—the fringe, if you will. Things the Federation can't dabble in for fear of overstepping boundaries."

"Like taking care of Felix Castile," Liesel guessed.

"Yes, exactly," Julianna affirmed.

"You know he was trying to take over a planet's population? Enslave them all?" Liesel said, scooping up the ferret and holding him protectively to her chest. "That's when I'd had enough."

Eddie nodded. "We know. Luckily we were able to stop him before that happened."

"Good," Liesel said, combing her fingers over the ferret's head. "I was locked up before that and didn't know what happened, and when they released me I had nowhere to go. Thankfully Logan gave me a job."

As if on cue the bartender hurried over with an empty tray. She regarded the three with a vicious expression and turned to Liesel.

"So?" Logan asked her friend.

"So I think they're telling me the truth. They want me as chief engineer," Liesel said.

"They're going to give you your old job back on that blasted ship? That good-for-nothing evil ship?" Logan asked.

"A ship is an organic being," Liesel explained. "It's neither good nor bad, but rather the product of the people on it and the places it travels. Just as intentions directly affect the body, so does a mission affect a ship."

"Would you stop spouting that mumbo-jumbo?" Logan shook her head, but still smiled.

"I'm just saying…" Liesel's voice trailed away and she suddenly became engrossed in petting her ferret again.

Logan turned to the three. "How do we know that you all are good and your missions aren't going to land Liesel back in jail?"

Eddie looked down the bar at Julianna, and she indicated Lars with a nod of her head. "Why don't you ask the Kezzin here? He can speak firsthand."

Lars coughed suddenly, as if flustered to be put on the spot. "Um…uh… The captain is… Well, our missions are good."

"Who are you to talk?" Logan asked, her chest held high.

"I'm Lieutenant Malseen, a pilot for Ghost Squadron," Lars stated, and his voice steadily grew more confident as he spoke. "When these two found me, I was a Brotherhood soldier who had been taken away from my family and forced to do whatever I was ordered. Since joining Ghost Squadron, I've helped free my people, brought vengeance against their abusers, and been reunited with my family."

Liesel stepped around Logan, who was again blocking her. "Wow, that's amazing."

"And it could be a bit fat lie," Logan said stubbornly.

Liesel shot her a measured glare. "How often do you see a Kezzin hanging around like this with humans?"

Logan let out an exasperated sigh. "Well, never, but it could still be a trap."

"It could," Liesel said simply.

"Do you even *want* your old job back?" Logan asked her friend, really grilling her.

Looking up at her with passion brimming in her eyes,

Liesel said, "I hated working for Felix, but I loved my work. I've missed it. The only thing I've wanted more was Sebastian back."

Logan seemed to struggle internally with this news, then a sort of smile twitched at her mouth. "Then you better get out of here before I change my mind and make you stay."

The door to the bar burst open and two Kezzin filed through, staggering as if already drunk. "Someone in here is in trouble," the first Kezzin yelled.

"There's a horde of Trids outside asking about a human and looking angry enough to split this place in half," the other Kezzin said.

Eddie whipped around to Lars, and Julianna was already on her feet. "Looks like those fucking shark-heads aren't so dumb after all. They tracked us here."

Julianna grabbed Lars by the arm. "Take Liesel through the back to the Q-Ship. The captain and I will take care of these fuckers."

"You seem like a good hard-working person," Eddie said to Logan, who was still staring at the drunks who'd announced the arrival of the Trids. "That's why we're going to take this fight away from your bar."

"Just keep Liesel safe or this momma wolf is going to rip your throat out," Logan said.

"You've got our word." Julianna pulled her pistol from her holster, giving Eddie the "let's do this" look.

He returned it with a wink.

One of the Kezzin from the back strode over, seeking to cut Julianna and Eddie off as they rushed for the door "What's going on?" he called to Logan.

"Some Trids are looking for Liesel," she yelled back. "These two are going to take care of it, though."

The Kezzin, who astoundingly was taller than Lars, appraised Julianna and Eddie. He laughed. "These horrid humans, you mean? What are they going to do, stomp on the Trids' toes and kick them in the shins?"

"I'll show you what I plan on doing, if you'd like," Julianna said, lowering her chin and regarding the half-drunk Kezzin with contempt. His buddies ambled up beside him.

"Why don't we take care of the Trids for you, little ones? We could use a good fight," the Kezzin said.

"You do owe it to Liesel," Logan said from behind the bar.

"Why don't we do it together," Eddie offered. "We might surprise you in how efficient we can be at kicking ass."

The Kezzin leader considered this, then nodded. "Yeah, watching puny humans duking it out will make me laugh for days. I'll play on your team, if you want."

"Then let's do it!" Julianna took the lead, storming out into the bright Kezzan sun. The brown desert spread as far as anyone could see, which made it easy to spot the approaching Trids. They were headed straight for the bar. The problem with that was the Q-Ship sat cloaked to the right of them. It was too likely that a brawler would knock into it. And how was Lars supposed to get Liesel into it if the fight took place right beside the ship?

There was only one solution. Julianna looked at Eddie

and he read her expression. *They had to bring the fight to the Trids.* They both sprinted to the left and drew the Trids after them. The Kezzin, who seemed in the mood for a good fight no matter who it was with, followed obediently. As Julianna expected, the Trid diverted their straight path and launched in their direction.

Because this was a no-fly zone since the Brotherhood had been disbanded, the Trids'd had to park their Stingrays on the other side of the border. *That was what happened when you didn't have cloaks,* Julianna thought, eyeing the Stingrays in the distance.

Ten Trids, as big as the four Kezzin behind them, stalked in their direction. Before they were close enough for a solid assault, they pulled their weapons and began firing. Bullets hit the ground, spraying dirt into the air.

Julianna dropped and rolled, firing back at the Trids, who made gigantic targets. She hit two, and they stumbled forward and fell hard.

Crouched beside her, Eddie fired several times. He hit two before having to reload.

"Guns are fancy, but fists are more fun," the leader of the Kezzin group said, not at all fazed by the bullets whizzing past him.

One of his men took a bullet to the arm and yelped loudly. This seemed to incite the Kezzin even more and they bounded forward, moving at a speed that Julianna hadn't seen from their species before. Their long legs propelled them rapidly to the Trids. Julianna darted to the side and fired to provide cover for the Kezzin. They closed in on the Trids, and the battle became a melee of fists and feet.

The Kezzin laughed as they fought. "You think you can come onto my planet and start trouble?" one of them yelled, and slammed his fist into the nearest Trid's face. The alien wavered before falling to the side. To the Kezzin's credit, they were making quick work of the Trids.

Julianna stood on the sidelines, a bit amazed by how well the two teams had worked together to take out a common enemy.

"And this should teach you to never pick on a lady," a Kezzin said, hopping into the air before slamming his foot into the abdomen of a fallen Trid.

Eddie tugged on Julianna's jacket. "I daresay they have this handled."

Julianna looked back to where the Q-Ship was hidden and parked. "Yeah, so we better make our exit before reinforcements arrive."

"I think these guys will demolish them if they do," Eddie said, laughing as the last Trid fell to the dusty ground.

23

Hatch's Lab, *Ricky Bobby*, Tangki System

"So you didn't screw it up," Hatch said, waddling over with the goggles he'd been working on.

"I know you had every expectation that we would, but this time we pulled through," Eddie said, standing proudly beside Liesel. Her ferret had perched on her shoulder and was sniffing the air wildly.

"You're Doctor A'Din Hatcherik," she said, looking him over in awe.

"Hatch," the Londil said, not giving her much attention. Most of his focus was on the goggles in his tentacles. "A'Din Hatcherik was my father, and although I'm a fine Londil I'm not him. Not even close." Hatch's eyes skipped briefly to the pair on the other side of his lab. Cheng and Knox sat across from each other on crates and exchanged nervous glances. *It couldn't be easy for them,* Eddie thought. Obviously they both wanted to get together again more than anything, but it would be a while until things felt normal, unlike for Liesel and Sebastian.

"The ship has changed a lot since I was Chief Engineer," Liesel said as she stared around at the cars in the lab area. "Is that a DeLorean?"

"That?" Hatch said, his tone a bit more sour than usual. "No, no. Don't you worry about that."

Liesel clasped her hands behind her back, chewing on her lip as she suppressed a smirk. "And I guess that's also not a Dodge Charger 440 Magnum, am I right?"

Hatch cast a quick glance over his shoulder at the yellow car. "Oh, no. That's definitely a Dodge Charger."

"You know, Hatch," Liesel began, "I wasn't born yesterday."

"I've read your file," Hatch said, tinkering with the goggles. "You practically were."

Liesel turned to Eddie and Julianna, who stood to the side. "Do you want me to resume my duties as before?"

Eddie shook his head. "No, not really. What we need you to do is get *Ricky Bobby* up to Federation standards. After that, you'll fall back into maintenance procedures. Hatch here can advise you on what we need, but his time has been monopolized by special projects, as you can see."

"Huh? Are you talking to me?" Hatch looked up, like he had been absorbed in his work. He was making a great show of being disinterested.

"I'd be honored to be advised by you, Hatch," Liesel said sweetly.

"Once you've had a chance to settle in, of course," Julianna added. "I'm guessing you might want to rest up and change."

Liesel looked down at her outfit. She was still wearing the flowing pants and jewelry from before. She shrugged. "Some rest and maybe a stretch would be good, and I've got a hankering for a smoothie, but I'm good in these clothes. It's how I'm used to dressing, although I daresay I'll need some new threads."

"We can get you outfitted with a jumpsuit," Eddie stated, referring to the uniform most of the crew wore. Not Hatch, for obvious reasons, and Knox preferred his threadbare jeans and t-shirt.

"Uhhh...I'd prefer something more flexible and light. I'm used to working in boho pants or yoga leggings," Liesel said.

"Right, well, I'm sure we can pick up something like that," Julianna said, her tone uncertain.

"And you must be starving. Hatch can show you where the cafeteria is. That will give him a chance to orient you," Eddie stated.

"I can't, actually. I'm busy." Hatch didn't look up from the goggles, his mouth hardly parting for the words.

"It's fine," Liesel said lightheartedly. "I remember where it is. That much couldn't have changed since I was aboard."

"Oh, that's right. Almost forgot that was why Hatch picked you for the position," Eddie said.

"Yes, and thank you, Hatch. I'm really honored that you wanted me for this position," Liesel sand.

"It's nothing," Hatch muttered. "It's only because you know the inner workings of the ship so well, and that will make the upgrades go a bit faster."

"Right, that makes sense." Liesel said, pulling Sebastian

from her shoulder. "We're ready to get to work, aren't we, my little buddy?"

The ferret pawed Liesel's nose, and Eddie noticed that Hatch did look up now with curiosity in his eyes. He'd watched those video logs of Liesel and had obviously seen something in her. Eddie guessed there was more to it than that she had previous knowledge of the ship. Even *he* had to admit that there was something about Liesel. She had a light about her, and Eddie was confident that she'd add to the good mood of the ship.

"Oh, before we forget," Julianna began. "We should introduce you to the ship's AI."

Liesel's mouth fell open. "No way. You have an AI?"

Julianna smiled. "Meet Ricky Bobby. He will help you with upgrades."

A squeal popped out of Liesel's mouth. "That's totally gnarly."

"Hello, Liesel. It's nice to meet you," Ricky Bobby said.

"Ricky Bobby, the honor is all mine!" Liesel spun in a circle as if trying to find him. "Hatch and an AI—it's like it's summer solstice!"

"Summer what?" Julianna whispered to Eddie.

He shook his head. "I don't understand half of what she's saying. Just smile and nod."

"Based on what I've deduced from watching your video logs, I've already alerted the kitchen staff to your dietary needs," Ricky Bobby said.

"Wow, that was very perceptive of you," Liesel said admiringly.

"I pride myself on my observational skills," Ricky Bobby said.

"Dietary needs?" Julianna asked.

Liesel smiled widely. "I'm a vegetarian."

"See!" Pip boomed overhead. "Someone who will finally understand me."

"Who is that?" Liesel asked, looking around again.

"That is the Commander's AI, Pip," Eddie explained, indicating Julianna. "Hatch has him interfaced so that he can communicate inside his lab."

"Two AIs? You've got to be kidding me," Liesel sang.

"I'm pleased to make your acquaintance too, Liesel," Pip said. "It's nice to have another level-headed person aboard."

"Did he just…" Eddie's voice trailed away as Julianna nodded.

"Yes, he likes to make those jokes," she said.

"I've been telling Julianna about all the health benefits of going vegan," Pip continued.

"Oh, well, I don't take it that far. I'm only a vegetarian," Liesel stated.

"We all have room to grow," Pip told her. "I've noticed an increase in energy and mental focus since adopting a vegan lifestyle."

Liesel turned to Julianna, a look of confusion on her face. "Isn't he…"

"Yes, but he likes to pretend," Julianna said.

"Don't you find that the brain fog has lifted since you've cut animal protein from your diet?" Pip asked.

"Uhhhh…yeah," Liesel agreed, suppressing a grin.

Julianna turned to Eddie with a look of mock seriousness on her face. "Do you know how you can tell if someone is a vegan?"

"How?" he asked.

"They'll tell you," she replied.

Knox sat on the edge of the metal crate, his gaze skirting the floor. There were some dust bunnies scattered around the boxes. Footprints covered the area, most of them Knox's. The sweep marks on the ground were most definitely from Hatch.

"C-c-can I say again how very sorry I am?" his father asked.

Knox forced himself to look up at the man, who sat across from him on a similar crate. His father now looked more as he remembered him, hair cut close to his head and freshly shaven. The wrinkles around his slanted eyes were deeper than Knox remembered, though, and the button-up shirt and slacks hung loosely on his bony frame. More disturbing than that was how he was sometimes there and then not, like he'd lost a part of himself.

"You don't have to keep apologizing," Knox stated, kicking his feet against the box. The action reminded him of being a child, but he'd lost his innocence long ago. One moment he had been his father's son and the next an orphan, left to fend for himself.

"B-b-but I knew better," Knox's father said, raw conviction in his voice. "If I hadn't used the Tangle Thief on myself I wouldn't have disappeared. I wouldn't have been abducted."

"The thing is, Dad, you don't know that."

Cheng looked up at his son, startled. "What do you mean?"

"I remember you constantly checking over your shoulder in those days," Knox began. "The Saverus were after you, and they might have gotten to you another way. Maybe you accelerated the process by using the Tangle Thief on yourself, but maybe it was inevitable that you'd disappear."

"Dom, you know that as a scientist I can't endorse the concept of fate. It's blasphemous to everything I believe in."

"'Knox,'" he corrected.

Cheng's forehead wrinkled like horizontal window blinds.

"'Knox' is my name now. I know it's strange for you, but will you call me that? Please?"

His father nodded, not looking entirely sure about the idea.

Knox ran his hand over his Mohawk, flattening it absentmindedly. "I know it's strange, but you have to realize that I've lived almost half my life without you. I'm not Dom anymore. That was the boy you knew, but you're going to have to...we're going to have to get to know each other all over again."

"Yes, I realize that, but I don't even know where to start," Cheng said.

"I think you're going to have to start by forgiving your-self for your mistake," Knox began, sounding older suddenly. "You deserted me. You didn't mean to, and I know if you could have made it back to me you would have. Dad, I don't blame you. I lived on the streets. I was hungry. Cold. Alone."

Cheng's face constricted oddly as he sought to hold back emotion.

"But you know what?" Knox asked, trying to suppress his own swelling feelings.

His father's eyebrows lifted as if to say, "What?"

"It made me who I am. I refuse to regret the past, because it made me who I am. It's taken me a hell of a long time to be proud of who I became." Knox blanched, not believing he'd cursed in front of his dad, but he swallowed the nervousness and continued, "Whether it's fate that took you away or a strange force that's brought us together, we should be grateful that we have the present moment. You have to stop living with regret."

"You've grown quite wise in these years," Cheng said, looking impressed.

"Dad, I survived out there because you raised me to be intelligent, resourceful, and hardworking. The things you taught me kept me going. You should be proud of yourself."

A pained smile spread across Cheng's face, and he looked out at the lab. Hatch was bustling around and talking to himself, as he often did. "Proud of myself? I think that's misplacing the credit. You endured out there in a cruel and unforgiving world. You found your way here, and earned an apprenticeship with the most talented scientist I've ever known. You've grown into a strong and capable young man." Cheng paused, and his gaze drifted back to his son's face. "I've never been prouder of anyone in my entire life, Knox."

24

Main Deck, *Ricky Bobby*, Tangki System

Fletcher's team stood in formation at attention. The Lieutenant, however, nervously darted his eyes between Julianna, Eddie, and the entrance to the area.

"I thought he'd be here by now," Fletcher said finally.

Eddie laughed easily. "He's Hatch. He does things on his schedule, not ours."

They'd been successful at closing Area One-Twenty-Six, but that couldn't last forever. It was an active facility that the Federation needed to access on a regular basis. Although General Reynolds had ordered that no one go into or out of Area One-Twenty-Six, that order would soon be terminated—which meant that Ghost Squadron had to secure the Tangle Thief and keep it safely away from the Saverus.

"It's fine," Julianna said calmly. "Area One-Twenty-Six will stay locked down until twenty-one hundred. We have plenty of time."

Hatch has just uploaded the directions to the Tangle Thief. I have access, Pip said in her head.

Good. We're ready to roll, then, Julianna confirmed.

Not quite, Pip stated as Hatch rounded a corner onto the deck. Behind him Knox carried a silver case.

Julianna tilted her head to the side, trying to understand what Hatch might be up to. He hurried over, pausing in front of them.

"I've sent the directions to both Pip and the captain's device," he began. "I think the fewer who know the location of the Tangle Thief, the better."

Eddie nodded, pulling his pad from his belt and scanning for the information. When he'd confirmed he had it he said, "I agree. Good move."

"We don't have sufficient time for me to brief you on everything you'll find in Area One-Twenty-Six," Hatch stated. "It's a confusing maze, with highly irregular and dangerous technology."

"Worse than Area Eight?" Eddie asked, looking impressed.

Hatch puffed out his cheeks. "Area One-Twenty-Six is where the Federation keeps some of the most classified projects—things that even God doesn't know about, and for good reason. He might condemn us all to hell for some of the things scientists came up with just to see if they could."

"I never took you for the religious type," Eddie mused.

Shaking his head, Hatch said, "Damn it, I'm not. But this is serious, so I'm trying to get your attention."

Eddie straightened, hiding a smile. "You've got it, Doctor."

"I appreciate the warning," Julianna offered, "but now that we have the directions, this should be an in-and-out job. Fletcher's team is only accompanying us as a precaution."

Hatch made a sound of frustration. "I'm afraid it's not that simple, Julie. Like I said, Area One-Twenty-Six is complicated. My directions may not be foolproof, since it's been almost ten years since I had the Tangle Thief locked up in the facility. Further, you're going to need to pass through several corridors to get there, and who knows what you'll find. I just can't account for all the variables with this one."

"If you're trying to get me excited for the mission you're doing a good job," Eddie stated.

Hatch rolled his bulbous eyes at the captain. "I'm trying to tell you that you're walking into something akin to the Outer Limits. Not everything in Area One-Twenty-Six can be contained, if you know what I mean."

Eddie scratched his head. "I don't, actually."

"And did you just make a reference to an ancient television show?" Fletcher asked.

"I've seen it," Eddie said. "It's pretty good."

Hatch cleared his throat. "Jaslene Corporation built the facility to ensure that what was inside couldn't get out. It's located far off the grid on Nexus, which protects others from the things it contains. However, once you enter the facility your proximity puts you at risk. Within the facility there are things that can penetrate the walls or transcend the space."

Eddie and Julianna exchanged tentative looks.

Hatch finally shrugged. "That's about the best information I can give you. I caution you to be careful, and question everything." He gave Eddie a warning look. "And don't touch anything."

"Except the Tangle Thief, right?" Eddie asked, jokingly.

"Let Julie handle that," Hatch said, waving a tentacle at her.

Julianna eyed the case Knox was holding with a quizzical expression. "Were you able to make the goggles work? Is that what's in the case?"

Hatch followed her gaze and shook his head. "No. As I mentioned before, I'm going to need a blood sample from a Saverus to make those work. I don't see any way around that."

Eddie gave Julianna a look of surprise. "Area One-Twenty-Six is shut down. Why are you worried about the Saverus? Sounds like we need to be more concerned with what's *in* Area One-Twenty-Six."

"The Saverus shouldn't be underestimated," Julianna said flatly. "How do I even know that you are you? They could have knocked you out when we were on Kezza, and this version of you could be an imposter." She waved her hand broadly at Eddie.

"You know I never left your sight, not even when we made a pit stop to drop off the pet shop of animals you risked your life to save."

"Are you ever going to let that go?" Julianna asked.

"Absolutely," Eddie chirped. "As soon as you give me something else to ream you about."

"If you two are quite done, I'd like to get back on topic," Hatch said, disapproval on his face. "Julie is quite right that the Saverus shouldn't be underestimated. I have every suspicion that we haven't seen the last of them, especially once the Tangle Thief is in your possession."

"Which means we need a way to destroy it pronto," Julianna stated.

"Cheng and I are working on that." Hatch turned to the case, unbuckling it to reveal row and rows of round green blobs. "I'm thinking that you need multiple eyes and ears in Area One-Twenty-Six to ensure you pick up on any funny activity, and this is the perfect opportunity to test Bob the Blob."

"Wait, it hasn't been fully tested?" Eddie asked, perplexed.

Hatch puffed out his cheeks diverting his eyes. "More or less. Honestly, the project got shelved after Cheng disappeared, so I'm not sure exactly how much the Federation did with it."

"But Bob is such a valuable tool. Why hasn't it been fully tested?" Julianna asked.

"Take a peek inside Area One-Twenty-Six and you'll understand," Hatch informed them. "The Federation isn't running short of technology to test, and Bob was considered a bit unconventional. Most don't immediately warm to the idea of sticking goo all over the place or on their person for spying purposes."

"I admit that it's not as glamourous as a chip for bugging would be, but I happen to like the unconventional aspect of it," Eddie said.

Julianna tended to agree with him. There was something better about having a spy that was alive and had telepathic abilities than a simple computer chip.

"Anyway, we're pretty certain that the bugs have been

worked out with Bob, but still be aware of anything that should be reported," Hatch stated.

Eddie laughed. "Bugs. Ha!"

"What should we be looking for?" Julianna asked.

Hatch picked up one of the blobs. "Accuracy. Transmission quality. Effectiveness of adhesiveness. Inability to detach."

"Wait!" Julianna exclaimed. "Are you saying that if we stick those on our body that there's a chance they won't come off?"

Hatch shrugged. "There's always a chance. That's the reason we test."

Eddie gave Julianna a commiserating expression. "Looks like we have just become guinea pigs."

"Fine," Julianna acquiesced. "We'll test them for you."

"Great." Hatch handed her one of the blobs. "I've activated three transmitters. The agents here," he swiped his tentacle at the case, "will send communications to these three. However, note that the relevant data will be divided, since overloading you three with the same information wouldn't be efficient. Instead, the transmitter will send the information to the person closest to the observation."

Eddie and Fletcher each took a transmitter, and each of them looked unsure where to stick the thing. Julianna had the same question, but finally stuck it behind her ear. If it never came off, at least her hair would cover it. The men followed her lead, placing the blobs behind their ears.

Knox shut the case and handed it to Julianna.

"I've created two dozen agents for you," Hatch said. "Place them anywhere you want spies."

"What happens when the mission is done?" Julianna asked. "Do we need to collect them?"

Hatch shook his head. "When you're done, the blobs will self-destruct at your command. There will be no noise or smell, and no remnants to show they were there."

"What about Bob?" Eddie asked.

"He generates more as needed," Hatch said.

"A renewable resource. I like it." Eddie sounded impressed.

Julianna handed the case to Fletcher. "Have your team distribute these throughout the area when they do their initial sweep."

Fletcher took the case and consented with a nod.

"All right, the next time we see you, Hatch, we'll have your Tangle Thief," Eddie said proudly, throwing his gaze in the direction of the Q-Ships, which were prepped and ready to go.

"Don't screw it up, Teach. If the Tangle Thief falls into the wrong hands, everyone in the galaxy will be in danger," Hatch said darkly.

Eddie gave Julianna a sideways look. "So no pressure, am I right, Commander?"

25

Area One-Twenty-Six, Nexus, Tangki System

Fletcher stared at the undulant waters of an ocean that he didn't know the name of. He liked geography. Maps. Knowing things. Knowledge was in fact power for the Lieutenant. He envied Julianna in that way, since she was constantly connected to a source of knowledge.

The ocean rocked into the sea wall, sending spray high into the air. The taste of salt tingled on the tip of Fletcher's tongue when he licked his lips. He began to whistle, because it calmed his nerves. No one could worry while whistling.

Fletcher's team waited until Julianna unlocked the main door into Area One-Twenty-Six. Unlike the other storage facility, this one wasn't located on a station but on a distant island on a relatively small planet. He put his back to the rolling sea, wondering when he'd see another body of water.

Although General Reynolds had ordered the facility

shut down until the Tangle Thief was located, some personnel had access. That was the reason Fletcher's team would sweep it, to ensure that it was secure. Hatch's speech about the dark mysteries that dwelled within the building had left Fletcher with a sense of foreboding, which put him on even higher alert.

Fletcher stepped past Julianna and Eddie, giving them a curt nod. Area One-Twenty-Six was much like the other storage facility, with brushed stainless-steel walls and sealed compartments down the long corridor. Fletcher had been given the blueprints for the facility and had devoured the information, memorizing the layout of the building.

Bluish lights that provided minimal visibility flicked on overhead as Fletcher marched forward, noting the crisp coolness in the space. When he opened his mouth, his breath misted.

On Fletcher's orders his team had divided into four to spread out through the facility and grounds. "Stay vigilant, and place the agents at even intervals. Report any suspicious activity."

The teams strode off, rifles in hand and every one of them on high alert. This team was probably the finest Fletcher had ever commanded. He'd worked with the best —proven men and women who'd inspired him with their self-sacrifice and bravery—but *this* team that he'd constructed worked as one in a way he'd never experienced before.

"Damn this place is confusing," one of Fletcher's team members said over the comm.

"Creepy as hell too," another replied.

"Just keep your chin up and eyes open," Fletcher ordered.

When he reached an intersection in the first hallway, information began to stream in from the transmitter blob behind his ear. The voice was a neutral male's and its pace was steady. "Second floor, southwest quadrant. Activity observed. The temperature is dropping. Currently at thirty-two degrees. Unknown object moving. Cannot make out details."

That didn't sound very ominous to Fletcher. *So the area was cold.* It was frigid throughout the building, probably the way they kept it to preserve...well, whatever was stored in Area One-Twenty-Six. Fletcher turned for the stairwell to check it out, though.

The other agents began reporting over the transmitter, but most of it was simple descriptions of their locations. Once they'd all checked in after being placed, the transmitters would only report if there was something deemed important. Apparently Bob's enhanced intelligence allowed him to distinguish relevant intel and give it to the right person. That meant he'd receive information that Eddie and Julianna didn't based on his location, and vice versa.

Fletcher paused at the top of the stairwell. It was as cold up here as it had been down below. He was still several yards from the agent's location when he noticed an archway that lead into a cove-like room. The hair raised on Fletcher's arms when he turned into the space. The temperature dropped significantly at the threshold and a blue glow lit the space, but its source wasn't obvious.

Sitting on a platform in the middle of the small space was a little tree—a bonsai, if he was remembering correctly. But it was different somehow, its branches distinct from each other.

A shadow moved behind the tree. Fletcher reached for his gun, spinning around, but there was nothing. When he took a deep breath, Fletcher's lungs burned from the cold. He felt like he was back on the ice planet of Klamath.

Behind him he heard a voice. No, not a voice. Whistling. He pivoted again, and finally he brought his gaze back to the strange bonsai. In the faint glow of the blue lights he noticed a sign next to the tree.

Family Tree.

Fletcher ignored the agent reporting more locations in his head and squinted at the plant. *Whose family tree is this?*

Compelled in a way he couldn't describe, Fletcher reached , his pointer finger extended. *Hatch said not to touch anything,* he told himself.

Fletcher was nothing if not a rule-follower. He pulled his hand back to his side as the whistling continued. Reflexively he straightened, looking around.

"You've grown to be strong," a woman's voice whispered from behind the tree.

Fletcher strode around it, but there was nothing there.

"Who said that?"

"But just like your father, you lost all your hair," the smooth voice said.

Fletcher froze. He knew that voice, and yet he didn't. Its origin was stuck in the back of his mind somewhere. He couldn't place it, though.

"Who are you?" Fletcher whispered.

"Child, we're not permitted to name names. It's one of the many rules," the voice said.

"Rules?" Fletcher asked. What *was* this thing? Where was the voice coming from?

"Oh yes, and you love your rules." The bodiless voice chuckled warmly. "Remember when I told you to ask for forgiveness rather than permission?"

Fletcher felt his eyes widen with shock. *It couldn't be.* His gaze fell to the sign next to the plant.

Family Tree.

"Grandma?" he whispered hoarsely.

Again she laughed. "I remember you told me that wasn't right. You wouldn't break rules, even when I was egging you on."

His ghostly grandmother continued to whistle, something she had done often. She'd been dead for most of his life.

Fletcher couldn't believe it. The voice distinctly sounded like his father's mother. She had been a rebellious old woman, always getting herself in trouble with her sharp tongue or her questionable schemes. He had loved her dearly.

"Are you in the tree?" Fletcher asked.

"Heavens no, child. That's ridiculous," his grandmother said. "I have no clue where I am, to be quite honest."

"If you're here, are there others too?" he asked, hoping.

"We're all here—everyone you're related to who has passed," Grandma Fletcher said.

Hot adrenaline coursed through Fletcher's arms, and he

pressed his hands to the pedestal where the tree sat, leaning over it. Suddenly his breath was warm spilling out over his shivering lips.

"Dad?" Fletcher asked, his voice shaking. "Are you there?"

Penrae took the binoculars from Verdok. She was having trouble focusing with the sea rocking underneath her. She was in the form of the crew member who had worked on this ship. Verdok had taken the role of the captain, not even giving her an option. Assuming the role of the captain had made it easy for them to take the ship from the harbor where it had been docked.

"I knew if we waited patiently they'd come for the Tangle Thief and lead us right to it," Verdok said, obnoxious pride in his scratchy voice. The captain, based on the constant coughing, had been in the salty ocean air too long and had a bad upper-respiratory infection.

Through the binoculars, Penrae watched as two guards flanked the entrance to Area One-Twenty-Six. More guards spread around the perimeter. For days it had been deserted. She'd grown weary of constantly being anchored to the same spot, watching the strange metal building sitting in the middle of a small island.

Verdok pulled the binoculars out of Penrae's grasp. "Tell the Petigren crew we're headed for land, and fast."

Penrae turned away from the bow of the ship. The Petigrens scrambled over the ship, their clawed feet scratching the deck as they scurried around with their shoulders slumped. She despised the rat creatures for some reason. Maybe it was because they had no sense of self-preservation, or because they all had a sniveling look in their beady eyes, as if trying to figure out a way to deceive at every turn.

"And Penrae," Verdok sputtered out, coughing. "When we go in, don't screw anything up like you did the last time."

Penrae gritted her teeth; well, the teeth of the human she'd shifted into. She didn't say a word, only strode off to give the order.

When the agents began reporting locations, Julianna and Eddie set off into Area One-Twenty-Six. The quicker they located the Tangle Thief, the better. Eddie wasn't afraid to admit that something creeped him out about the storage facility, and that was saying a lot. He'd met the foulest aliens in the galaxy and frequented dives that would make most shiver with disgust.

He followed Julianna down a corridor, knowing she saw the map with Hatch's directions in her head. If they got separated he had the instructions on his pad, but he hoped it didn't come to that.

"Hey, let's stay together while we're in here," Eddie said, striding through the frigid blue-lit hallway. It felt like they were walking through a refrigerator, which only increased the fright factor.

"Because?" Julianna asked.

"Because I have a feeling separating will only lead to confusion and chaos."

Julianna made a sharp turn and trotted down a set of stairs that led to the basement. The hallway the stairs emptied into was exactly like the one they'd come from. It was lined with doors and crisscrossed by multiple other hallways.

"This place *is* a maze," Julianna observed.

"Just as Hatch said." Eddie gave her a meaningful look. "Stick together, cool?"

She nodded, the dim blue light casting dark shadows under her eyes and nose, making her look ominous.

"What was it again? Right, second left, two rights, and two lefts?" Eddie asked, trying to remember the directions.

"And then third right," Julianna confirmed, her gaze to the side like she was focusing on the map projected in her retina and not the daunting stretch of hallway in front of them.

"Okay, we got this. Let's do it," Eddie stated, ignoring the agents listing their locations in his head. It was easy enough to send them to the back of his mind, like static he could ignore. He wondered if that was what Julianna did with Pip when she couldn't pay attention to him.

"There's our first right," Julianna stated, striding forward. It was roughly ten yards down the seemingly never-ending corridor. The intersecting hallways, Eddie noticed as they passed one on the left, weren't Ts. Instead they cut across this hallway at strange angles, making them harder to spot in the dim lighting. *You'd think the Federation would invest in better lighting in their storage facility.*

"Are you able to ignore Pip?" Eddie asked, for some

reason needing to fill the silence. It was a strange thing for him to need, since he was a person who valued silence and required much decompression time. Most wouldn't have guessed that based on his outgoing personality, but that was just the thing. Extroverts expended a lot more energy, and needed much time to recoup.

Julianna's eyes were full of laughter when she gazed at him. "I wish. He's pretty…persistent."

"Is he always talking?" Eddie asked, not sure why the AI intrigued him. It must have been the prospect of being integrated with him, and also giving him control of his body.

A sadistic smile crossed her lips. A conversation was transpiring between the two now, he could tell.

"What is Pip saying?" Eddie asked, curious.

"As usual he's talking smack," Julianna said. "And although it feels like he never shuts up, it's about like what you experience with Ricky Bobby or ArchAngel. He's quiet, but always there."

Julianna laughed suddenly.

"What did he say to that?" Eddie asked.

"He keeps threatening to get a life of his own," Julianna responded.

Eddie tucked his head back on his neck, confused. "How would that work?"

"Exactly the same way an AI would put on a pair of shoes. They wouldn't." Julianna stopped at the first right.

"Here's our first turn," Eddie stated, noticing how eerily quiet it was. He'd expected to run across one of the Special Forces soldiers, but it appeared strangely deserted.

Julianna started forward, then halted, grabbing Eddie

by the forearm. He looked at her and then to where she was pointing. Five feet back the way they'd come was another hallway.

"Wait, is *that* the first right?" Eddie asked.

"I think so," Julianna stated. "This would be the second."

Eddie looked between the hallway in front of them and the one behind them and shook his head. "Was that there before?"

Julianna sighed. "Of course it was. We were just distracted and nearly missed it. No more talking. One wrong turn and we're screwed."

Eddie scanned the area with a discriminating glare. "I don't know. I don't trust what I see in this place."

He could have sworn that a moment ago there were more left hallway intersections. After making a full rotation, he noticed that Julianna was wearing a similarly paranoid expression.

"Maybe one of the protections Jaslene Corporation uses is visual illusions to confuse trespassers," she stated.

Eddie nodded minutely. "That would explain this."

"Come on, let's go." She grabbed him by the arm again and led him to the hallway they'd nearly missed.

Not surprisingly, this hallway looked exactly the same as the others. Where were the doors or compartments, like in the other facility? How could there not be units? This was a storage facility, but it felt like a catacomb of confusion.

"What? I did what I thought was right. Get over it," Julianna stated, looking back at Eddie with an incredulous expression.

He halted. "I didn't say anything."

"Yes, you did."

Eyes wide and unblinking, he gave her an expression that said, "You're losing your damn mind."

"Eddie, I heard you just now."

"What did I say?" he asked.

She growled and charged off faster.

"Eating a meal with you can be highly annoying," Julianna stated matter-of-factly.

Eddie paused, wondering if he heard her right. "What does that have to do with anything?"

Julianna whipped around. "What does what?"

"My table manners. I get that I ate all the dip without asking when we were at that pub on Kezza. I apologized already."

Julianna's face was covered with confused outrage. "Why are you bringing that up right now?"

Eddie took two steps and leaned into her. "Because you just threw it up in my face. You're obviously still mad."

She laughed. "I didn't bring it up. And speaking of being mad, you're the one still pissed about me risking my life for the bunnies."

"What? I'm not either. Why would you say that?" He did think that about the animals, but had promised to let it go.

"Because you just brought it up again," she said in a tight whisper.

"No, Jules, I didn't," Eddie stated.

They both paused, their eyes moving to the side. When their gazes connected there was a new intensity in them.

"Something is messing with us," Julianna said.

"It's in our heads," Eddie said in a hush. "How else would it know that stuff?"

"And it's trying to make us fight."

Eddie realized now exactly what Hatch meant about this place. He'd faced danger, explosions, bullets, and mortal peril, but nothing like this—a mind-fucking-game.

"Okay, we have to stay where we can see each other's mouths," Eddie instructed. "That way if I don't see you talk but hear your voice, I know it's not you."

"Or we split up," Julianna offered.

"NO!" Eddie said, his voice louder than he'd expected. He sucked in a breath, trying to stay calm. This place had him more flustered than he would have thought possible. It was dark, cold, and confusing. Well, and it had weird science magic that messed with their heads. This proved that sanity was easier to lose than most realized. Only a few factors drew the line between stable and crazy.

"I just don't think it's a good idea to split up. Too much could go wrong, and we're both trying to accomplish the same thing," Eddie said, his voice full of conviction.

Julianna nodded. "Although I'm unsure how we're supposed to find the Tangle Thief if we're staring at each other."

Eddie sighed. "Good point. Maybe we just have to ignore the negative things we hear."

Julianna raised an eyebrow, giving him a challenging look. "You sure you've got thick enough skin for that?"

Eddie scoffed. "Of course I do. I'm a real man, Jules."

She nodded, unconvinced. "Fine, let's try that and hope this fight instigator leaves us alone soon." Turning around, she sighed and said, "Because we're already lost. I think we passed our turn. Let's backtrack."

Eddie agreed with a nod, leading off.

"Your lack of knowledge of alien cultures is incredibly embarrassing. I wished you'd brush up on that," Julianna said loudly at his back.

Eddie continued to march forward. *It's just an entity trying to fuck with us,* he told himself.

"Oh, and if you offer me unsolicited advice on my flying again I'm going to kick your ass," the imposter Julianna stated.

Eddie ground his teeth. What if this fucker was pulling out the things they really felt and hadn't said? The complaints they were too afraid to voice?

"Everyone thinks it's cute, but you can be incredibly immature," the impersonator said.

Eddie couldn't help it. He halted, clenching his fists by his side. "Enough!" he boomed.

"Hey, dumbass! You're going the wrong way," Julianna said from behind him.

Eddie spun around, expecting to see Julianna standing there. She wasn't. The hallway was empty.

26

Area One-Twenty-Six, Nexus, Tangki System

Penrae, in the form of a crew member on the shore, waved her hands overhead. They'd intentionally docked on the back side of the island where the Special Forces soldiers were fewer. One of the men in uniform ran through the sparse trees, his rifle in hand.

"You can't land here," the soldier yelled, slowing as he neared. "This island is closed to outsiders.

"Right, I get it," Penrae said, her voice deep. The man she'd shifted into was stocky and smelled like fish and sweat. "I saw the no trespassing signs on the way in, but I didn't have a choice." Penrae threw her meaty arm at the ship, which appeared empty since the Petigrens were below decks. "My ship hit something and I need to..." Her voice trailed away as she caught sight of another soldier pushing through the trees.

"Kendrick," a woman in uniform said. "It's all right. I gave him permission to dock."

The man turned around. "You what? Nona, you heard the Lieutenant's orders."

"I know, but the boat is wrecked. What else is he supposed to do?" the woman said.

The soldier named Kendrick shook his head. "I don't know. I'm calling this in. The Lieutenant needs to know about it." He lifted his hand to his ear, but before he made contact the soldier behind him pulled up her weapon and shot him twice in the back. Shock filled every feature on the man's face. His mouth fell open. His hand pressed into this chest where one of the bullets had exited. He stumbled. Fell. Landed face-first in the sand.

Penrae wasn't granted a moment to experience the remorse that welled up inside her.

"Grab his arms and drag him into the water," the woman soldier said. Her appearance didn't deceive Penrae. She'd recognized the way Verdok spoke to her. Like she was beneath him. He'd apparently managed to sneak up to the facility and gain the identity of one of the soldiers. They only had to be in close proximity to take on someone's appearance.

She did as she was told, finding the job of pushing the dead man's body into the sea exceptionally easy in her current form.

"Assume his identity. We don't have much time," Verdok barked.

"I think you meant to say 'please,'" Penrae said bitterly.

"What did you say?" he asked, his voice high-pitched but with the normal heat still present.

"Nothing," she said, shifting into the form of the male soldier. The timing couldn't have been better, because just then two more soldiers sprinted through the trees, worry flecking their faces. Penrae cast a look behind her. To her relief, the body of the soldier had drifted out with the tide and was probably bobbing behind the boat. Still, they didn't have too long before it materialized on the other side.

"We heard gunshots," the first said. "Are you all right?"

Penrae nodded. This body was much cleaner than the previous one, and easier to tolerate. "We're fine. I think they came from over there." She pointed to the bank on the far side of the island, away from the entrance to the facility. "We're going to search this boat. It was just discovered."

The other soldier, a young male, stepped forward and looked at Verdok's form, perplexed. "Nona, what are you doing down here? You're stationed at the entrance."

"I ran over, same as you," Verdok said, injecting confidence in his tone. Penrae had to hand it to him. He knew how to pull off a role, never giving a hint that he was an imposter. "You two check out the disturbance on the other side of the island. I'm going to report this to the Lieutenant."

That had apparently been the right thing to say, because the two soldiers nodded and sprinted in the opposite direction. When they were a safe distance away, Verdok shifted into the form of the young male soldier. He didn't grant Penrae another look, only strode toward the entrance to the storage facility. "Bring the Petigrens. It's time to get what we came for."

Nona straddled the tree's thick branch. She'd dreamed of climbing trees when she was a little girl. Dreamed of making a fort in one, and writing poetry there during the day and crafting imaginative ideas by night. Then she'd curl up with her flashlight and book and read under the stars until her eyelids were too heavy and she fell fast asleep in her treehouse.

Never did she think that she'd grow up to climb trees with a sniper rifle in tow and stand guard, waiting to pick off bad guys.

Sometimes we think we know what we want out of life. Tree-houses and poetry. Nona sighed at the long-ago dream. It seemed almost comical. The one time her family had gone on a camping expedition, climbing trees hadn't been on the itinerary. She was handed a pistol and told, "It's time to learn how to shoot."

Thinking back, there had never been another path for her. Nona was a soldier. A marksman. A sniper. And she was the *fucking best.*

She aimed her scope toward the entrance to Area One-Twenty-Six, scanning as she'd done regularly for the last hour. Standing watch could get tedious, but boredom was her worst enemy.

"Only the boring get bored," her mother used to say. She probably didn't realize that those words would save her daughter and many others. Nona still crafted poetry and dreamt of imaginative ideas in trees as she had once hoped to do, but now she did it while holding a M24. The ramblings of her imagination kept her alert, and that kept others safe.

Nona brought her scope to the left and caught two

figures, Donny and Kendrick. *What were they doing off their posts?* she wondered.

Nona was about to zoom in when she caught activity behind them. She pressed the scope harder into her eye. *Fuck!*

She swept the scope to the left, taking in the strange sight. Roughly ten yards behind Donny and Kendrick were a dozen or more rat-men like the ones they'd fought in Area Eight.

Did Donny and Kendrick know they were about to be ambushed? Nona could pick off a few of the rat-men, but how many before they overwhelmed the rest of her team?

She pulled back slightly, blinking away from the scope. Wait. Could they be? It didn't make sense that Donny and Kendrick were someone else—that someone had stolen their identities. When would they have had a chance? That would be as bizarre as someone having stolen her identity while she was perched ten feet up in the safety of the tree.

Nona pressed the scope to her eye again. In the ten seconds she'd taken to make sense of what she was seeing the rat-men had taken over, running past Donny and Kendrick. The men did nothing as the creatures ran past them.

They were shapeshifters, Nona realized. She released the safety. Got Donny in her sights. And then he disappeared. He had shifted into the form of a rat-man. She scanned the crowd of beasts as they sprinted for the entrance of Area One-Twenty-Six. Kendrick was gone too. They were charging the facility.

She pressed the button to activate the comm. The Lieutenant needed to be alerted right away. Then she'd join the battle that was about to ensue.

Fletcher's hands shook. He couldn't believe this. All these years after losing his father, he finally had a chance to say the one thing that had been stolen from him. He was going to get closure. Finally he'd have a chance to tell his father that he loved him. His death would feel final, because Fletcher would have gotten the gift of saying goodbye.

Too often the day his father had left and didn't return played in Fletcher's head. It still didn't feel real. For years he had believed that his father would show up again. That was what had happened for that mechanic, Knox. Why couldn't it happen for Fletcher? But he knew better. He'd read the reports. Cornel Fletcher was dead, and had been for some time now.

"Dad? Are you there?" Fletcher asked, speaking to the Family Tree. He realized that it was the source of the faint blue light.

"He's here," his grandmother said. "Give him a moment. Takes him longer to come through."

"Dad!" Fletcher yelled. "It's me! Chad!"

The comm crackled in his ear. "Sir, this is Officer Fuller," Nona said in a mad rush. "Those rat-men are back, and there's two shapeshifters. I had them in my sights but they disappeared."

Fletcher stumbled back. "What? How did they get through the perimeter?"

He turned for the corridor and then back to the Family Tree.

"I don't know, sir, but they are rushing the entrance."

The sound of gunfire echoed over the comm.

"The rat-men are running straight at Brady and Jordan at the entrance," Nona said. "I'm trying to hold them off, but there's so many of them they're going to get through."

"Fuck. I'm on my way. Send Jamison and Hunter over from perimeter," Fletcher said. He stared longingly at the Family Tree. Why hadn't his father come through? What was keeping him?

Fletcher blinked at the tree for another moment, but he couldn't waste any more time. He was his father's son, and that meant that he arrived early to a fight and defended his territory. Spinning around, Fletcher sprinted down the long corridor back the way he'd come.

He'd made it to the first floor when the transmitter said in his ear, "Second floor, southwest quadrant. A male's voice is yelling the name "Chad.""

Fletcher wasn't allowed a moment of regret, because the fight had indeed begun. The entrance to Area One-Twenty-Six was being overwhelmed by Petigrens.

Julianna knew it had been wrong to run off from Eddie, but that thing, whatever it was, was trying to cause a fight between them. They were better off parting. And he'd gone past the next turn because he wasn't paying attention.

She was overly controlling on missions! How dare he say such a thing? Well, he hadn't, but that thing had and she was pretty certain that whatever-it-was read their thoughts. How else would Eddie have heard that bit about table manners?

It did irk Julianna that every time they went anywhere Eddie ate the communal food like it was all his. He'd eat the last eggroll without asking first. Take all the ketchup. Pick up the center bowl of salsa and empty it onto his plate. It was just fucking inconsiderate. She was secretly glad that wicked paranormal creature had told her secret. Eddie needed to know that he was a pig at the table. Maybe now he wouldn't steal her fries and say "yoink," like it was funny instead of fucking irritating.

You don't think you're being a little uptight on all this? Pip asked.

No, Julianna snapped, turning a corner.

She could think and find her way now that she didn't have to listen to Eddie tell her how she didn't take enough leisure time or shouldn't hold everyone else to her personal standards. She'd find the Tangle Thief on her own, then she'd blacken Eddie's eye. Because even if he hadn't voiced these complaints, he'd thought them.

You're partners. You weren't supposed to leave him behind, Pip reprimanded.

I didn't. I just got lost, Julianna lied.

Table manners are a big deal for me too. Can you tell Lars that not everyone needs to see what he's eating while he's eating it?

No, I'm kind of busy at the moment.

Later, then.

Busy then, too.

You're in the worst mood I've seen you in for a long time.

I'm trying to find a fucking deadly weapon in a maze.

And you've been heavily criticized by someone you care about.

Was I? I don't remember.

Julianna took her second left, stomping the entire time. Only one more right to go and she'd be there. She'd made significant progress—finally.

It doesn't feel good when someone special is rude to you, is that it?

Pip, are you trying to make inferences?

I wouldn't dream of it. I'm simply saying maybe you know how I feel now.

I'm sorry, I thought being rude to each other was our thing.

Only because you've built this fortress around yourself and the only thing that can get over your walls is a humorous volley.

So you want me to be nice to you, is that it?

Pip was quiet for a long moment. No. Nice is Marilla's thing, and it's how I see Knox. Even Lars, sometimes. I like you the way you are.

Then why are we having this conversation?

Because you do your best work when I distract you.

"Motherfucker," Julianna whispered. Without having to even think about it and while lost in thought, she'd found her way to where the Tangle Thief was supposed to be located.

Damn it, Pip, you're one heck of a guy.

Thanks, Jules. I think you're swell too.

Julianna pulled her access badge from her pocket as the

transmitter broadcasted in her head. "Front sector. Main entrance," it said. "There's a disturbance. Approximately, fifteen Petigrens have attacked Ghost Squadron and are forcing their way into the facility."

"Fuck," Julianna exclaimed, pressing the comm button. "Fletcher, you read me?"

Silence.

Julianna tried again. "Fletcher? Teach? Do you copy?"

Nothing.

Now that Julianna thought about it, Eddie could have contacted her as soon as they had separated, but he hadn't.

Pip, what's going on here?

I'm looking into it. There appears to be something causing interference with the comm in this section of Area One-Twenty-Six.

I'm not surprised with all the wacky shit down here. Can you fix it?

Yes, but I'm not sure how soon.

Julianna paused in front of the unit where the Tangle Thief was. They were under attack, and she'd lost Eddie. Nevertheless, she had to get what they'd come here for.

"Fregin, can you hear me?" Eddie asked over the comm for the tenth time.

Still he got no response.

He could hardly believe she'd deserted him. Maybe she'd gotten lost, he'd tried to tell himself. He didn't believe it, though. Julianna had, like him, heard one too many things that she didn't like and gone her own way. Eddie almost couldn't blame her. It sucked to hear only the things a person *didn't* like about you.

Why couldn't the strange entity have told Julianna how her laugh made him laugh? Or that she was the strongest person he knew? Or even that more than a couple of times one of her speeches had hit him in the chest with its power? Instead she'd only heard the bad.

Eddie turned down another corridor, completely lost now. The map on his pad was useless, since he didn't know where he was. GPS would have been brilliant, but since the comm didn't work down here it was hard to believe that anything else like that would.

"Basement. Northeast quadrant," the transmitter said in Eddie's head. "A woman has entered the main corridor."

"Julianna?" Eddie asked, hopeful.

"Quick scan shows that individual meets the Commander's height, build, and physical characteristics," the transmitter said.

"Bob, can you help me find her?" Eddie asked.

"I can direct you to the agent that is spying on her," Bob said through the transmitter.

"Great, because I'm fucking lost," Eddie told it, incredibly glad he'd taken that green blob from Area Eight.

27

Area One-Twenty-Six, Nexus, Tangki System

The only thing that could have kept Fletcher from his father was the news that his team was being overrun by Petigrens. He slid to a halt to find the entrance to Area One-Twenty-Six in complete chaos. Loud screeching yells erupted from the doors.

Brady and Jordan were stationed outside the entrance, their backs to Fletcher. Brady was on the steps, firing nonstop. Jordan stood several feet to the right and was trying to keep the growling rodents back.

Fletcher arrived at the entrance and looked over Brady's shoulder at a scene that filled him with disgust. The rat-men charged forward, many of them climbing over the dead bodies of their own to get into the facility. One dove forward several feet and rammed into Jordan, knocking her down. Her gun flew from her hands.

The monster scratched her face, snapping and trying to bite her. She rolled over onto it, throwing hard punches into its face. Fletcher knew he couldn't get off a shot at the beast without risking Jordan.

"Fuck! Where did these come from?" Fletcher asked Brady.

"I don't know!" he yelled over the constant gunfire. "They're spread out and just keep coming."

Fletcher caught something in his peripheral vision. He moved to the side of Brady, aiming his rifle as he did. Three Petigrens had snuck around the other side of the building and were trying to gain entrance while Brady was forced to fend off attacks from the right. Fletcher fired several times, but the aliens kept coming. They were tough as fuck to kill.

He steadied his weapon. Aimed. Fired once. The bullet went straight through the head of the closest Petigren.

Fletcher said over his shoulder, "Shoot for the head if you can."

"Yes, sir!" Brady yelled.

Fletcher stabilized his weapon, taking aim at the next Petigren. It was on all fours, its teeth chattering angrily. At the side of the building Fletcher caught a movement. He fired, killing the Petigren, then chanced a glance at the far wall.

He caught sight of Nona helping Jamison, who had his arm slung over her shoulder. He was limping. Hurt.

Fletcher directed his sights at the final Petigren approaching on that side and shot once. The beast fell, dead.

"Come on," Fletcher yelled, hurrying the two forward.

Once this side of the entrance was clear Nona sped up, nearly dragging Jamison. His head was to the side, he was close to passing out. Fletcher relieved Nona of him as soon as she had him at the steps, and pulled the wounded soldier into Area One-Twenty-Six and to the far wall.

Looking him over, he didn't see any injuries. "What happened to him?"

Nona was panting hard. She pulled her rifle from across her back, her gaze on the entrance where the battle was still going strong. "He got stuck on the perimeter. I couldn't get to him in time. I left my post too late."

Fletcher ran his eyes over Jamison's limp form. There was no blood, no puncture wounds, no broken bones—but Jamison was breathing. He didn't get it, but he'd have to tend to the man later.

He turned back to Nona, about to rise when the butt of her rifle slammed down on the top of his head.

Julianna held the security badge up, taking a deep breath.

She paused. Dropped her hand by her side.

This felt wrong. She shouldn't be stalling, but she didn't want to go into this room for some reason. Well, she didn't want to go in *alone*.

This is stupid, she told herself. *The squadron is under attack. I came for a job, and I must complete it.*

Again lifting her hand to the reader, she tried once more. The badge didn't read on the scanner. She swiped it again.

"You have to turn it sideways," Eddie said from behind her.

She spun around. He hadn't come from the same

hallway as she had, but rather was on the other side of her. Julianna nearly choked on a breath.

"How did you get here?" she asked, flattening herself into the doorway. Maybe he was a Saverus.

"I'm not a Saverus," Eddie said like he was in her fucking head. "Bob led me here."

"Bob…" Julianna mused, wondering if there was a way that the Saverus could know about Bob. "How did he do that?"

Eddie pointed at something behind Julianna on the wall. She narrowed her eyes in the dim corridor. There on the wall, she made out the familiar small green blob stuck discreetly in place. "He had his agent help me."

Julianna looked Eddie up and down. "It's really you, isn't it?"

"Yes, and you *really* deserted me," he said, sounding hurt.

"I… Yeah, I guess I did," she said, not even trying to lie.

"I guess I get it. We can face so much, but when we're confronted with emotions we want to flee."

Julianna found herself smiling. "You know, you can be kind of poetic when you want to be."

Eddie shrugged. "I know, but the thing is, usually I don't want to be." He reached out and took the card from her and held it at an odd angle. "The readers, I noticed, work better if you hold the badge like this."

Julianna watched as Eddie ran the card through the security access. It buzzed once, and the door slid open.

They were finally in.

"Oh, and the comms are out," she said in a rush. "But Pip is working on them."

Eddie nodded. "Yes, I tried them."

"There's been an attack by the Petigrens," she stated.

Eddie straightened. "Which explains why you thought I could be a Saverus at first."

"And which is also why we need to grab the Tangle Thief and get the fuck out of here."

Eddie waved an arm forward. "Shall we do it together, then?"

Julianna consented with a nod. "Yes, let's."

They rushed into the large room. The walls were lined with hundreds of numbered lockers. The Tangle Thief was in 2858—straight ahead, second row from the bottom according to Hatch.

Julianna had taken one step forward when something went completely wrong. A force like she'd never experienced pushed her to the ground. There was something wrong with the gravity in the room.

* * *

Nona picked off two rat-men who had Jordan cornered again. She'd finally begun to make progress, thinning the crowd of angry giant rodents. The beasts were hard to take down, but a well-placed shot knocked the fuckers off fast. The problem that was their heads were covered in bushy hair and they had large ears, making it hard to be precise. One might think that a large target would make it easy, but not when the shit-holes had tiny rat brains. Nona had quickly learned that a bullet to the head didn't always ensure a kill.

She was about to pick off a snarling rat-man who was

whipping his tail around madly and looked to be close to leaping at Brady. The beasts could run fast and jump farther than she would have expected, which was why they were nearly at the entrance to the facility.

She froze as she looked at the other side of the building, where two figures had emerged. *No, that's impossible,* she told herself. Through her scope she watched as the Lieutenant fired, taking out two rat-men. They fell, and then he turned and helped two figures into the building. Two people who looked exactly like her and Jamison.

Underneath her she heard scratching, so she flipped her head down. One of the disgusting beasts had found her position and was climbing up the tree after her. It clawed at her boot and she scrambled up, trying to find her footing in the tree. The rat reached for her, wrapping its clawed paw around her boot. He was surprisingly strong and yanked her hard to one side. Nona grabbed a nearby limb, trying to keep her rifle from falling to the ground.

The rat-man sank is teeth into her leg, and scorching pain rocketed from her calf all the way up to her hip. Nona yelled and yanked her leg free, then pulled her pistol from her holster. Shot once.

The fucking rodent fell to the ground, blood spraying from the bullet wound in his head.

Nona fumbled for the comm button. "Lieutenant! It's Nona. Do you read me?"

There was no answer.

Holstering her pistol, she ignored the blinding pain in her leg and swung herself around onto the trunk of the tree, siding down to the ground, rifle in hand.

"Lieutenant Fletcher, this is Officer Fuller. Do you copy?"

Again, silence.

Nona didn't think, she only reacted, sprinting on her injured leg past the half-dead rat-men on the ground.

Area One-Twenty-Six, Nexus, Tangki System

Every part of Julianna was weighed down by a crushing force. On hands and knees, she felt unable to move, like she was cemented to the floor.

"The gravity in here must be high," Eddie said, seeming to struggle with each word. He was also crouched on the floor.

"How is that possible?" Julianna stated, looking around. They were at the front of the large room lined with lockers. Was this a super gravity chamber? That didn't make sense. The door to the corridor was still open.

"I think wondering how anything makes sense in Area One-Twenty-Six is a waste of brain cells." Eddie indicated with his head in the direction of locker 2858. "Think we can make it over there?"

Julianna tried to lift her hand but the overwhelming weight made it nearly impossible. She managed to slide her palm forward an inch but the effort was instantly exhausting.

"Damn it!" she shouted. "This is going to take forever."

"I think it's going to wear us out before we make it over there," Eddie said, his breath heavy as he inched forward beside her.

At the side of the room, something emerged through the wall. Julianna craned her head the best she could and gazed at the strange ghostly figure. It was a woman... No, not quite. She had the facial features and curves of a woman, but this was definitely an alien. Her head was bald, and she bore strange markings on her face and arms. She shimmered blue all over, and her transparency made her details hard to discern.

"Who are you?" Julianna asked, struggling to stay in the tabletop position. Her midsection felt close to crumbling to the floor from the constant downward pressure.

The alien looked at Eddie and Julianna as if she had just noticed that they were pinned to the floor. It was strange that the super gravity didn't seem to affect her. Well, as strange as anything else in Area One-Twenty-Six. "I see that the gravity storm has shifted. It was overdue, I suppose," the strange alien said.

"Storm?" Eddie asked. "That's what this is?"

"Yes, it moves throughout Area One-Twenty-Six randomly," the alien said, calm superiority in her voice. She flickered, disappearing and then becoming visible again.

"How do we get out of it?" Julianna asked.

"You ask," the alien said simply.

Julianna sputtered a cough. That seemed ridiculous, but

welcome to her present reality. "Ummm...storm, will you let us go?"

The alien shook her head minutely. "I meant me. You ask me."

"Oh," Eddie said, sounding as surprised as Julianna felt. "Will you help us out of this gravity storm?"

"Please," Julianna added for good measure.

The alien lifted her three-fingered hand and directed it at Julianna and Eddie. She expected to fly to safety, but instead Julianna entered sudden blackness. There was nothing. She blinked, and still she saw blackness. There was only silence. Her body was frozen. She was just about to call to Pip when she materialized on the ground next to the far wall of lockers.

Breathless, Julianna spun to find Eddie right beside her.

"What happened?" Julianna asked him, but he had no answers. He scanned his body as if making sure it was all there.

"You asked for help, so I teleported you away from the gravity storm," the alien said coolly.

"Thank you," Julianna said, staring around. There was no way to tell where the storm started and ended.

Wow. No species that she was aware of could teleport. Whatever this alien was, she was incredibly powerful.

"Will you be so kind to teleport us out when we're done?" Eddie asked.

The alien turned to the wall she'd come through as though about to leave. "I only offer one favor to strangers."

"Wait, wait, wait," Julianna said in a rush. "Who are you?"

What she really wanted to ask was, "What are you?"

However, that was usually considered rude among alien cultures. This woman wasn't the typical alien they had found the galaxy. She might even be atypical for her race.

The alien stopped and faced them. "You may call me 'Kyra.'"

"I'm Julianna, and this is Eddie. Do you live here, Kyra?"

She blinked, her large almond-shaped eyes impassive. "I dwell here, more like. As you might have guessed, I'm neither alive nor dead. I'm in-between."

"I hadn't actually guessed that," Eddie said, mystified.

Julianna cast her eyes at the entrance. She expected the Petigrens or something else to be charging this way at any moment. Without any communication with Fletcher and his team, she felt cut off. The only thing that made her feel any better was that the gravity storm would provide a bit of a buffer should something rush in there right then.

"Why do you dwell here?" Julianna asked, her curiosity getting the better of her.

Kyra looked around, judging the space. "I do not fit into the world anymore. When offered the opportunity to reside here, I accepted."

"And do they study you in return?" Julianna asked.

"They might try," Kyra said simply.

The transmitter clicked in Julianna's head before stating, "Near your location, two figures approach, both moving quickly."

Julianna spun to Eddie and a look of caution sprang to his face. He'd heard the transmission as well. Simultaneously they pulled their weapons from their holsters, but Julianna knew she couldn't fire. The bullet would be ineffective as soon as it hit the gravity storm.

She tensed at the sound of running footsteps. Whoever was approaching was about to come into view.

Eddie's mind reeled with options for how to fight whatever was approaching. A gravity storm posed all sorts of hurdles, and he and Julianna were in essence stuck in this room. He glanced behind him momentarily. At least the Tangle Thief was close by.

Two figures ran past the door to the room, then immediately backtracked.

Fletcher and Kendrick halted in the archway, breathless.

Eddie's blew out a breath and relaxed slightly. "Lieutenant, what's going on? The comms are out."

Julianna glanced at Eddie. "Pip said he's working on it. He has a fix. It appears that a signal blocked the radios."

Fletcher, with Jamison by his side, started forward. "We've fended off the Petigrens."

"Stop!" Julianna commanded.

Fletcher halted, throwing out a protective arm at Jamison, a question in his eyes.

"There's a gravity storm of some sort between the door and us," she stated. "If you step in here you're going to get caught in it."

Fletcher's face registered his alarm.

"The storm will pass within moments. It doesn't like this space," Kyra said from beside them.

Fletcher face twisted with confusion at the sight of the alien.

"Well, that's good news, because we're going to need a way out of here," Eddie said.

"In the meantime…" Julianna turned toward the lockers at their backs. There were no handles, and the seams were barely visible.

"Right, but do you remember how we open the locker?" Eddie asked. He dared to look at Kyra, but she wasn't paying attention. Her focus was on the men by the entrance.

"I'm sure there's a reasonable solution," Julianna said. She stooped, squinting at the unit marked 2858.

A sudden thought occurred to Eddie, and he revolved to face Fletcher. "How did Hatch say we were to open these lockers, Fletcher?"

Julianna shot a look of confusion at Eddie, but he tried to silence her with a covert eye movement and she understood at once. They needed to ensure Fletcher wasn't a Saverus.

The Lieutenant scratched his head. "If he said something about it, I don't think I heard."

So far, so good. "Right, maybe he didn't then." Eddie tried to think of another trick question quickly.

Before he could, Fletcher said, "My transmitter just reported that we have someone approaching from the north side."

Eddie and Julianna had heard this too, and they both relaxed minutely. He was the real Fletcher if he had the transmitter. He had to be, which meant that they'd have to trust that Kendrick was the real person too.

"None of the Petigrens have gotten into Area One-

Twenty-Six, correct?" Eddie asked, watching Julianna mess with the storage locker.

"No, and the guards I stationed outside are still there. None have come in or out," Fletcher replied.

"That's exactly what I needed to hear," Eddie said with a sigh of relief. He noticed now that Kyra hadn't left. She was watching them with mild interest.

Julianna pushed hard on the unit, but it didn't budge. She pried at the edges to no effect. "I don't get it," she said, grunting with frustration. "How does it open?"

"Hatch should have told us that. He conveniently left out that detail," Eddie said, amusement in his tone.

Julianna sighed and poked at the metal plate in a last-ditch effort. The drawer slid out from the gentle movement, opening fully.

"Ha-ha!" Eddie shouted, victorious. "It's one of those 'slightest touch' sort of things."

She smiled up at him, triumph in her eyes, but when they looked down they saw something they weren't expecting.

"I-I-It's empty!" Eddie stammered.

Julianna looked all around the drawer, even checking the back. She ran her hand over the top and sides, but found nothing.

"What's going on?" Fletcher called.

"The drawer is empty," Eddie said, running his eyes over the units beside the open one. "Maybe we have the wrong locker."

"What?" Fletcher yelled. "How is that possible?"

Eddie shook his head. "I don't know."

Julianna stood. "I think it's the right locker. Hatch said the Tangle Thief was in Unit 2858."

"And it was," Kyra said coolly.

Julianna spun to face the strange alien. "What did you say?"

All eyes were on the ghost-like figure. "The item you are looking for was in that unit—I will tell you that much."

"Did you take it?" Eddie asked.

Kyra appraised him. "I cannot pick up objects. You might have noticed that I pass through them."

"Right, so who took the Tangle Thief?" Julianna asked. "Was it the Saverus? Did you see someone recently come in here and steal it?"

Kyra cast her eyes at Fletcher and Kendrick before letting her gaze fall on Julianna. "No, the device you seek was taken many years ago, I believe. Time does not pass the same for me as it does for you, but I think it's been close to a decade now."

"A decade!" Eddie yelled. "It's been gone for that long?"

"Hatch said that the items in here are kept locked up unless special orders are given. They are too dangerous to even risk updating an inventory list," Julianna stated.

"Do you know who took the device?" Fletcher called from the far side of the room. He looked ready to pounce on something.

"Yes. I was standing right over there when it happened." Kyra pointed to the other side of the room, which was exactly like this side. It was just a nondescript line of lockers.

"Who?" Julianna asked, buzzing with anxiety. "Can you tell us who took the Tangle Thief?"

"I cannot. I did not ask his name," Kyra said, a misty quality to her voice. "He asked me if I'd help him, and I did."

"Help him?" Julianna didn't know what to do with this information. The Tangle Thief was gone! Well, it had been gone for a while. It was out in the galaxy somewhere. They had to find it.

"As I did with you two, I help all those who ask one time," Kyra said flatly.

She was too calm in this situation, which called for immediate answers and lots of them.

"What did you help him do?" Eddie asked, sounding much steadier than Julianna felt.

"He asked me to send him someplace safe, so I did," Kyra replied.

"Where did you send him?" Fletcher asked, his voice dripping with urgency.

Kyra gave him an unhurried look. "A place that is safe only remains that way while no one who is a potential threat knows about it."

"We're not a threat. We're here to help," Julianna urged.

"And besides, that was over ten years ago," Eddie argued.

"I'm programed with certain laws, and one is to keep my word," Kyra stated.

She was a hologram! Now Julianna understood. A hologram with incredible powers. It made sense that she could teleport, because she was a projection herself.

I've almost got the comm back online, Pip said

Thanks, Julianna said quickly.

Give me fifteen seconds and you can contact the team.

Okay.

"Can you tell us anything about where this person with the Tangle Thief went?" Eddie asked, pressing for more information.

"I cannot tell you the safe place I sent the boy because that would go against my programming," Kyra stated. "All I can say is that my teleportation abilities are confined to the planet on which I reside."

"Did you just say 'boy?'" Julianna asked.

"A boy took the Tangle Thief?" Fletcher asked in disbelief.

"Yes, a boy with a black Mohawk," Kyra answered.

Area One-Twenty-Six, Nexus, Tangki System

Julianna's gaze connected with Eddie's, and both had shock written in their eyes. That Knox had removed the Tangle Thief was unfathomable. It couldn't be true. He would have told them. He was the least deceptive person that they knew.

Julianna shook her head. "You must be mistaken. That's impossible."

"I do not make mistakes," Kyra said.

She wouldn't, either, Pip informed Julianna. **If she is programmed she's not subject to mistakes, and all her information is stored accurately.**

But Pip, this doesn't make any sense.

"This boy," Eddie began. "How did he get here?" He pointed to the floor.

"He just appeared, much like how I teleport," Kyra answered.

"Was he holding a similar device to the one in the locker?" Julianna asked, starting to piece it together.

Kyra nodded. "Yes, and the drawer sprang open when he arrived."

Julianna's mouth fell open. She looked at Eddie. "Because he was entangled with the receiver located here."

Eddie understood at once. "He used the client his father left behind in the house."

"Probably in a desperate attempt to find Cheng," Julianna said, completing his sentence.

"And when Cheng's receiver was destroyed, the client somehow became entangled with the one here that Hatch had made," Eddie said in a rush.

"We'll have to ask Hatch if it's possible to entangle more than two particles," Julianna said in a hushed voice, thinking.

"Of course it's possible!" Fletcher said, his voice irate. "What does all this mean? Where is the Tangle Thief?"

Julianna raised an eyebrow at Fletcher. *He could know about entanglement,* she reasoned. She ignored him, trying to piece all this together.

"We don't know," Eddie said, sounding as bemused as she was. "This is a mystery. We'll need more answers."

"What we need is the Tangle Thief," Fletcher nearly yelled. He spun around to face Kendrick. "It's here on this planet. She said so."

"Wait, what are you—" The static of the comm interrupted Julianna.

"Captain? Commander? Do you read me?" a voice said over the comm. "This is Officer Fuller."

"Yes, Nona, we copy," Eddie said at once.

"I'm trying to locate you," Nona said, sounding out of breath. "We've had a breach."

"Oh fuck," Eddie stammered. "Lieutenant Fletcher said that the premises were secure."

Fletcher looked up at the mention of his name. He'd been having a hushed conversation with Kendrick.

"Sir, Lieutenant Fletcher has been knocked out. He's unconscious," Nona stated.

Everything slowed down for an instant. The hum in the room grew indistinct and the space suddenly turned suddenly frigid. And then just as quickly the situation shot into fast forward.

Eddie yanked his gun from his holster and aimed it at Fletcher. The imposter froze facing Kendrick. His eyes darted to the side. He knew he was caught, but the real question was regarding the gravity storm. Eddie couldn't shoot if it was still up, and they all knew it.

In his peripheral vision, he caught Julianna's movement. She tossed something into the air. But why? And then he saw it. She'd pulled a bandana from her pocket and thrown it in front of them. It puffed up on release and floated to the ground normally, not immediately yanked down like they had been.

The storm was gone!

Eddie fired straight at the imposter, but he grabbed Kendrick and drew him in front of himself, using the soldier as a shield.

The bullet struck him in the shoulder and the Saverus

discarded Kendrick Jamison and ran in the opposite direction. Eddie didn't hesitate, tearing after him, but he found the hallway empty.

"Bob, where is the person who just fled from this corridor?" Eddie asked.

Julianna, he could tell from a quick glance, had stayed behind to tend to the injured soldier.

"Take your second right. He's headed for the stairs," the transmitter said.

"Shut down the main exit and secure the perimeter," Eddie ordered into the comm.

"We're low on forces, but can secure the main entrance," one of the Special Forces soldiers answered over the comm.

Damn it! Eddie couldn't let this damn Saverus get away —he knew too much. And the pair of them had knocked Fletcher out. They were going to pay. He whipped around the next bend and rammed straight into someone.

Nona covered her nose from the assault and looked up at Eddie, confused. She'd been running too.

Eddie lunged back, aiming his weapon at the young sniper. "Hands in the air."

Nona immediately complied. "I'm not one of them, I promise. I just radioed you to tell you Fletcher was knocked out."

Wasn't that what the imposter would say? He had been there for the exchange, and he obviously had access to everything Fletcher did if he'd heard Bob's transmitter before.

Eddie sucked in a quick breath. What was he supposed to do? Detain this soldier? What if she wasn't the real

Saverus and he lost the chance to get them? Did he let her go?

Too many questions raced through his head in that moment. "Turn around and march forward," Eddie stated. Nona complied, hands in the air.

Just then he heard a door slam by the exit stairs.

"Figure fleeing," someone said over the comm.

"Fuck!" Eddie roared, darting around the person he realized was actually Nona. "Follow him! Don't let him get away."

"Roger that, captain," the voice called.

"Another wave of rat-men has been deployed," a separate voice called. "We're being attacked again."

Hell-fuck-damn. Of *course* the shitfaced Saverus had an exit strategy. Send the Petigrens in waves to get them into and out of Area One-Twenty-Six.

"We're going to have to retreat inside the facility," a voice said over the comm. "We don't have enough forces to defeat them."

"This is the captain," Eddie said over the comm when he reached the stairs. "All forces report to the main entrance. I want you to take these fucking rats down and do it swiftly."

It might be a challenge, but they had the power to defeat another attack—although Eddie realized that it was only a diversion so that the fucking Saverus could escape. Damn it. There was no chance he was going to get to him if he had to fight through the Petigrens. Still, he'd help the team defend themselves. That Saverus' day would come.

Eddie was about to bound up the stairs when he heard something over his comm that made him freeze.

"Captain, I think you should return to the storage units," Julianna stated. "There's something you need to see."

Thanks to Bob's transmitters, Eddie was able to easily find his way through the maze of Area One-Twenty-Six. He'd asked Julianna what he needed to see, but she had said it was better if he saw with his own eyes.

Eddie was at his max with surprises for the day. *Knox.* It was fucking Knox who had taken the Tangle Thief. Or he'd had the device, but who knew where it was now? Nothing made sense in this place. *Nothing.*

When Eddie returned to the hallway where the storage units were located, he didn't have to wonder long what Julianna wanted him to see. It was sprawled out across the floor of the corridor and incredibly difficult to miss. Where Kendrick's body had been lay something scaly.

He didn't stop until he was right beside Julianna, and he stared down at the massive red snake.

"So that's a Saverus?" Eddie asked. Blood oozed from an upper section of the giant reptile. It was as big around as his waist, and at least fifteen feet long. Its eyes were shut, and its forked tongue protruded from its mouth slightly.

"Yes, and it isn't dead," Julianna stated.

"This one was impersonating Kendrick," Eddie guessed.

"Yes, and the other one used it as a shield," Julianna stated.

"So much for loyalty among the Saverus." Eddie toed the thing with his boot. Looking at the scaly snake made Eddie want to recoil with disgust. It had taken a while to get used to Lars' lizard features, but he had arms and legs and resembled humans more than the reptile he was related to. This thing…it seemed purely snake, and yet it had the ability to become anyone it desired. It was so much more than a snake, and that was creepy as hell.

"I think we should take it with us," Julianna said, breaking the silence.

Eddie looked at her in horror. "You've lost your damn mind. I think we should kill it."

She shook her head. "Hatch needs a blood sample."

"Then we take a sample and drown this thing in the ocean," Eddie stated coldly.

"But what if it knows something? I mean…it has to, right? It's a Saverus," Julianna argued.

"You forget that it can become any of us," Eddie replied.

"I didn't forget that, actually," Julianna said.

"So you want to take this thing aboard *Ricky Bobby* where it can impersonate any of the crew, causing confusion and havoc?" Eddie asked.

"We'll put it in the brig. There's no way it can get out of there even if it pretends to be you or me."

Eddie considered this for a moment.

"We don't have the Tangle Thief," Julianna continued. "We have a bigger fucking mission ahead of us now, and a lot of serious unknowns. We're going to need every advantage we can get, and one of them could be knowing why the fuck the Saverus want the Tangle Thief in the first place."

"Because they are coldblooded demons," Eddie stated through gritted teeth.

"Well, this passed-out demon can tell us, but only if you help me load it into the ship," Julianna said.

Eddie considered this for a moment. He didn't like the idea of putting this shapeshifter on the ship, and almost more disgusting was the idea of picking it up. However, he had to admit that since they'd lost the other Saverus, they needed to shift the odds into their favor. He leaned over and reached for the tail, hoisting it over his shoulder. "Yeah, fine, but you're carrying the fucking head."

Jack Renfro's Office, *Ricky Bobby*, Tangki System

Knox didn't understand why he'd been called to the spymaster's office. He'd seen Jack Renfro around the ship, but he'd never talked to him one-on-one. The man smiled warmly at Knox as he welcomed him in. He was smartly dressed in a button-up pinstriped shirt and dark slacks. Like Knox's father Jack wore his black hair back, but there was an edginess to the younger man's hair, similar to how he'd seen Superman wear his in those comic books from Earth.

Knox tried to smile when Jack held out a welcoming hand for him to shake, but it turned into more of a cough. He nearly choked when Jack stood back to reveal Eddie, Julianna, Hatch, and his father inside the office.

"Come in, Knox," Jack said, waving him into the room. "Have a seat." He motioned to a high-backed chair covered in red velvet.

Knox had never been anywhere this nice. It was filled

with fine art and statues, and he felt out of place in his frayed jeans and faded t-shirt.

"Go ahead, Gunner," Hatch said, waving a tentacle at the seat. "We're not going to bite. Just need to ask you some questions."

Since the crew had returned from Area One-Twenty-Six, there had been a lot of whispering but no real information. Apparently, they'd brought back a prisoner who was in the brig, but no one was allowed near it. And many of the Special Forces soldiers were being treated in the infirmary for bite wounds and other injuries. One had been killed. Whatever had happened in Area One-Twenty-Six, it had been dark and brutal.

"Knox, you're not in trouble," Eddie stated matter-of-factly.

Knox's eyes darted back and forth, sweat beaded his forehead and gripped the arms of the chair until his knuckles turned white.

He tried to swallow. Failed, and let his mouth partly open to take a breath.

"Son," his father said, sitting down on the sofa next to the chair. He leaned forward. "Do you remember ever being on the planet Nexus?"

Knox didn't have to think about that. He'd only been on four planets, and two of those had been with Ghost Squadron. "No, never."

Hatch and his father exchanged looks.

"Think really hard, Dom…Knox," Cheng said, correcting himself before using the wrong name.

"Nexus is a planet rich with life," Julianna said. "There's lush trees, and clear waters. Does that ring any bells?"

Knox shook his head. "I've never been to Nexus. I was born on Ronin, and I ended up on Planet L2SCQ-6 on the frontier."

"Yes," Hatch said, stoking his tentacle absentmindedly over his mouth as if musing on the idea. "How did you end up on that planet out on the frontier?"

"Mateo found me," Knox explained. Why were they having this conversation? This was old news. Why should the unimportant details of his childhood matter?

"Mateo found you *after* you were on Planet L2SCQ-6," Jack interjected.

Knox blinked. "Yeah, I guess he did."

"Do you remember how you ended up there?" his father asked. "It's a long way from Ronin."

Knox tried again to swallow. Why did his throat feel like it was closing? "I don't know," he heard himself say. How could that be true? How could he not know how he'd gotten to the planet when he'd spent a huge portion of his life there?

The others exchanged nervous glances.

"I don't know. I just sort of..." Knox's voice trailed away.

"Sort of what?" Eddie asked, his tone gentle and his eyes kind.

"It sounds weird," Knox began. He didn't want to speak the truth. They wouldn't believe him.

"We're used to weird," Julianna said, her voice light. "Go for it. Tell us."

It bolstered his confidence. "I don't know. It feels like I just sort of woke up there." A laugh tumbled from his mouth. He was sure everyone would laugh with him, but they didn't. The room fell silent, and Julianna glanced at Eddie. Hatch gave Jack a wide-eyed look.

It was Knox's father who leaned forward and placed a hand on his son's knee, giving him real contact. "Son, do you remember what happened before then? Before you ended up on the frontier?"

Knox squinted down at the fancy carpet under his feet. He *didn't* remember. The more he tried to remember his past, the farther it seemed to retreat from his grasp. How was it that he'd never wondered how he'd gotten from Ronin to Planet L2SCQ-6?

"I'm sorry, I don't," Knox said, feeling nearly breathless now. His head swam with dizziness and he pushed back into the seat, thinking he was going to pass out. "Is there a reason you're asking all these questions?"

Of course there was a reason, Knox thought, and he didn't think he'd like the answer very much based on the serious expressions on everyone's faces.

Hatch cleared his throat. "Do you remember exactly what you did after your father disappeared?"

Finally, a question that Knox could answer. He let out the breath he was holding. "Yes. When I came out of my room, Dad was gone. I checked the kitchen, the bathroom, his room, and his office, and I couldn't find him anywhere." That memory was vivid as anything he could remember.

"And then what did you do?" Jack asked.

"Well, then I..." Knox's voice trailed away, his head suddenly tight. "Then...I..." He couldn't remember. How could he not remember?

He looked up at his father. "I left. You were gone and I knew I was in trouble, so I left."

"Where did you go?" Hatch asked.

"I-I..." Knox began, but he had no answer. Hatch was looking at him intently, and the last thing he wanted to do was lie to the scientist he respected so much. "I don't remember. Honestly, I don't remember anything after I checked the house."

"And then you ended up on Planet L2SCQ-6, is that right?" Julianna asked.

That couldn't be right, Knox thought, and yet he didn't have anything to fill in the missing pieces. He nodded. "Yes, that's all I remember. I'm sorry. I'm not lying, I promise."

Hatch reached out a tentacle to pat Knox on the shoulder, then paused with his limb hovering an inch from the boy. He pulled it back. "No one thinks you're lying, kid. We're just trying to figure out what happened."

"What do you mean, what happened?" Knox asked.

Eddie scooted forward on the sofa so that he was perched on its edge. "When we were in Area One-Twenty-Six we discovered that the Tangle Thief had already been taken."

Knox's shoulders slumped with defeat. This was horrible news. "Oh, no. I'm sorry. What happened?"

"Someone took it years ago," Eddie continued. "We spoke to a hologram who told us that she'd helped this person. She sent him, along with the components of the Tangle Thief, to safety somewhere on Nexus."

Knox narrowed his eyes in confusion. "How could she do that?"

Cheng cleared his throat. "Similar to the Tangle Thief but with limited capacity, this hologram has the power to transport, it seems."

"Wow," Knox whispered. The things around this place kept getting stranger. "How are you going to find the Tangle Thief?"

"That's why we're talking to you," Hatch told him. "It appears that the person who took the Tangle Thief was you."

Static seemed to fill Knox's ears. He stared around the room, the faces looking at him blurred. There was an intoxicating perfume in the office which sought to choke him. Everything was too much. This was a dream. Knox had to wake up.

He bolted to his feet. "Me? It couldn't have been me!"

Cheng was on his feet a moment later. "It's okay, Knox. We've figured it out, and it absolutely was you."

Knox looked at his father, puzzled. How could this be okay? How could Knox have been the one to take the Tangle Thief and that was fine? "I didn't do it!"

"You're the only option," Jack said, coming to stand next to him. He set a comforting hand on his shoulder. "When your father was gone, you tried to find him. The client device—the other part of the Tangle Thief—would have been in the house, but it wasn't found when the area was searched. Neither were you. We can deduce that you used the Tangle Thief, hoping to find your father. Hatch has confirmed that with your father's receiver destroyed you would have been redirected to the Tangle Thief he created, which was stored in Area One-Twenty-Six. You met Kyra the hologram there, and since you were scared, you asked to be transported to some place safe on Nexus. That much we've been able to deduce. What we have to find out is how you ended up on Planet L2SCQ-6."

"But more importantly, we need to find out where you hid the Tangle Thief," Eddie stated.

"How do you know I did?" Knox asked.

"Because you're smart," Hatch said at once. "You would have known that the technology was dangerous, and it was why your father was being stalked."

Knox turned to his father. "But you said that using the Tangle Thief on humans was dangerous. If I used it then…"

"You were young," his father said consolingly. "It appears to have caused you memory loss, which is why you can't recall what happened between the time you were on Ronin and when you arrived on Planet L2SCQ-6."

"Oh," Knox said, sitting back down in the chair. His legs felt too heavy. It seemed that every part of him was weighted with lead.

"Knox," Eddie said thoughtfully, "we think you can help us to find the Tangle Thief."

Knox's head bolted upright. "You do?"

Eddie nodded. "It's going to take a lot of work, though."

Knox didn't mind work. He preferred that to not knowing. "What can I do?"

"The memories are stored in your mind, but we're going to have to unlock them," Hatch said. "If you're willing, we're going to try to break through whatever is preventing you from remembering what happened on Nexus."

Knox took a breath, and was finally able to swallow. He looked up at his father with an expression he hoped showed the courage he felt in his heart, although his hands were shaking. "I'll do it. I'll do whatever it takes to help you find the Tangle Thief."

31

Infirmary, *Ricky Bobby*, Tangki System

Whatever they'd given Fletcher to soothe his aching head, he wanted more of it. He wanted to overdose on the stuff so he could fall back to sleep. Anything was better than sitting on this bed and staring out at the world, knowing he'd missed his chance.

The transmitter reported that his father had called his name from the Family Tree. He'd been so close...so close to telling him that he loved him. Telling his father that he missed him. Saying that final goodbye. And the moment had been stolen from him.

He laid his throbbing head back on the pillow. If he'd known he'd be knocked out by a fucking Saverus, he would have stayed and spoken to his father. Regret filled his insides like sludge.

However, he knew that if he hadn't shown up to help his team he'd have other regrets. There was no winning in this situation.

Fletcher had failed in so many ways at Area One-Twenty-Six. Kendrick was dead. One of his men. A part of his team.

Yes, he'd heard his father's voice, but that had only made things worse. Now he knew that on Nexus was a device he could use to talk to his father. He had to get back to it. He had to tell his father that his life's goal was to avenge his death and kill the pirate who had murdered him —that Rosco would die by Fletcher's hands. After delivering that final promise to his father, he'd tell him goodbye and achieve the closure he'd always wanted.

Bridge, *Ricky Bobby*, Tangki System

"You want to talk about the things we heard our imposter selves say in Area One-Twenty-Six?" Eddie asked Julianna, staring straight ahead like the strategy board held something of great interest. He was deliberately not looking at her, and they both knew it.

"You mean the criticisms that some alien spouted to try and make us fight?" Julianna clarified.

"I suspect they were true. Do you really think I have awful table manners?"

Julianna shrugged. "It's not the worst problem a person could have."

"I'm willing to go through etiquette classes if it will make you happy," he said diffidently.

Julianna laughed. "I can totally see you walking around with a book on your head and drinking tea with your pinky in the air."

Eddie blanched. "Why would anyone do either of those things?"

Julianna smiled. "To make themselves more proper."

Eddie's face held mild disinterest. "Oh, I've never been good with customs, but if it will make me more tolerable then I'll do it. I don't deny there's a gap in my education."

"Right, I get it. We all have room for improvement," Julianna said, pretending to study the strategy board as well.

"I think you're right, that I need to brush up on alien cultures," Eddie stated.

Julianna couldn't hide the look of surprise on her face. "Damn, that alien was busy spouting information."

"Yes, and I can only worry about what it said to you from me."

"Not much, since I'm pretty flawless, but maybe I could work on my control issues a bit," Julianna confessed.

"Thanks. You're always so willing." Eddie smiled. "And I'll put my napkin in my lap and keep my elbows off the dining table."

Julianna waved him off. "Actually, I'd just settle for you not putting your chicken bones on the table when you're done with them like it's a trashcan."

Eddie nodded. "Fair enough."

"How is the prisoner?" Julianna asked, referring to the Saverus they'd captured.

Eddie yawned loudly. "It's still in the infirmary being treated for the bullet wound. Last I heard it was heavily sedated."

"I'm anxious to interrogate that Saverus. I hope that he

or she or whatever it is will be helpful for us," Julianna related.

"The important thing is Knox is on our team. He's going to be how we locate the Tangle Thief," Eddie said, chewing on his lip. He opened his mouth and hesitated.

"What?" Julianna prompted, sensing he wanted to say more.

"I know I gave you shit about taking the prisoner, but it was probably a good idea. I mean, maybe," Eddie said, giving her a wink.

"We have the upper hand when we know the most about our enemy."

Eddie yawned again, his eyes watering. "Yeah, I know. Those damn snakes just freak me out." He looked at Julianna with a mock serious expression. "Would you have rescued them if it had been caged snakes on Kai, or just fuzzy little bunnies?"

"Back to that again?" she asked, perturbed.

He shrugged, a bit of his former irritation surfacing on his face.

"Are you ready for this mystery adventure, tracking down the Tangle Thief?" Julianna asked, relieved to change the subject.

"Yes and no," Eddie said yawning. "Give me five hours to catch some sleep and I'll be as bright eyed as a bunny."

"I think you could have used another reference," Julianna said as Eddie headed for the exit.

"I bet you do," he said over his shoulder. "When I return, I'll be as a chipper as a mouse—like the ones you risked your very life to protect."

"Get over it, Teach," Julianna shot back.

"Not yet, Fregin," he retorted.

Julianna allowed herself to chuckle when Eddie was gone.

I have a confession to make, Pip stated with an awkward laugh.

Julianna paused. She was at her limit with new information for the moment. *What?*

I actually don't think we should go vegan.

We? What, do you have a rabbit in your hat?

No, we let them all go on Kezza. You should have let me keep one, though.

I'm not even giving that request any attention.

Anyway, consuming animal products is probably best, since we exert so much energy and need our protein, Pip reasoned.

We? Ha-ha. And I was never going vegan.

I'm looking into the paleo diet now. It involves eating only foods—

Pip, you've officially driven me insane, she said, cutting him off.

He let out an audible sigh. **Ok, then, mission accomplished. I'm going to go take a nap. I'm exhausted.**

Julianna rolled her eyes as she yawned. Tomorrow was another day full of missions that would seek to break them, villains who would no doubt try to elude them, and Pip, who would probably succeed at annoying her. She silently smiled to herself as she made her way to her personal quarters.

Julianna couldn't wait for tomorrow, but tonight she'd rest.

EPILOGUE

Verdok stood under the bright spotlight inside the Council chambers. The elders perched on their benches behind their tall walls, looking down at him.

He was in trouble, and he knew it. If Penrae were here, maybe things would be different. Maybe he could convince them that she'd screwed up everything—but for once she wasn't present to take the blame she undoubtedly deserved.

Verdok didn't wonder where Penrae was. The Council of Elders didn't seem very concerned either. They all knew she wouldn't talk. To betray the Saverus was one of the worst crimes. And like the rest of them, Penrae had undergone the sacrificial rituals that bound her to secrecy.

Betrayal of the Saverus would cause her great pain. She would suffer for eternity. That was what the elders had taught them, and Verdok believed it. All Saverus believed it. This doctrine was as old as the planet Savern where they'd originated, and to which they'd one day return.

"Verdok, how do you plead?" the head Council member asked.

Verdok hung his giant head, his tongue flicking quickly in and out of his mouth.

"Guilty. I'm guilty of failing in my mission."

The head Council member seemed to loom larger, his eyes narrowing. "The sentence for a guilty plea is death."

Verdok tensed all over. If Penrae was here... "Wait! I did learn details of where the Tangle Thief could be. I'm your best hope for locating the device."

The head Council member considered this. "That's true, but you lost many Petigrens in this mission."

"Petigrens who wanted to help the cause," Verdok argued. Why was this even an issue? Petigrens bred so fast and frequently that replacing them was of no consequence to the Saverus.

"Although that might be true, you have failed and must be punished," the head Council member said.

"I'm not arguing that," Verdok said in a rush. "Just give me a chance to fix things. I know if given another opportunity, I can redeem myself."

Many of the Council members leaned forward, menace heavy in their scrutinizing eyes.

"We need to know what you plan to do to make up for this unsuccessful mission," the head Council member demanded.

Verdok lifted his head, injecting confidence into his every move as he swayed back and forth hypnotically. "I plan to scour the planet Nexus. If you grant me the resources, I'll follow every lead until I discover where the boy with the black Mohawk hid the Tangle Thief. And having met our enemy, I'm in the best position to fool them, shall we meet again."

The Council muttered amongst themselves, a barrage of hissed words.

"Silence," the head Council member said, looking straight at Verdok. "You make a good point and you did bring us this information, so I'll grant your request and spare you this time. But one more failed attempt and your sentence will be carried out."

Verdok swayed more so now. "Do not worry, Elders. I will not let you down. I will find the Tangle Thief and deliver it to you so we can have what we've long dreamed of."

FINIS

I grew up the youngest of four children and let me just tell you something straight. My siblings were assholes. My oldest sister thought that television was the devil. I wished I were kidding when I said that. If she caught me watching it then she pulled me by my hair and thrust me out into nature. My brother hogged the television so he could make himself feel worthy by playing Mario Bros and trying to beat those nearly unbeatable castles. And my other sister was addicted to Lifetime television and most of our quality time together consisted of watching the movie of the week where some needy woman faked a pregnancy for attention. Am I going somewhere with this? Eventually...

My point is that unlike most children, I wasn't handed a remote and allowed to pick what I wanted to watch. Oh no. My life was complicated from the start. So instead of free-choice television, I'd usually wonder into my mom's room where she was watching the older generation of

Doctor Who. Oh, yes, I'm *that* old. *Oh, good,* you're probably all thinking. *Author girl has a fucking point now.*

Yes, I do. I grew up watching Tom Baker as the Doctor, running around and being an amazingly eccentric character. Most can't pinpoint when they fell in love with science fiction, but I can. I can also thank my asshole siblings for modeling me into who I became. Some complain that they are victims of their childhood. I'm the product of a bunch of bullies and proud of it. If allowed to watch my choice in programming then I may not be obsessed with British television. I might have actually watched a Disney cartoon and then where the hell would I be right now?

And I digress.

It was important to me that I make this arc an homage to one of the best shows in history. I'm a huge fan of the new generation of Doctor Who. Before I started writing I actually would watch David Tennant as the Doctor and think, *I want to write something as smart as this.* Actually, I think the Matt Smith seasons are really the smartest, but I'm opening another can of worms. My point is that I took inspiration from the series and stuck it straight into these books.

Okay, I owe many thanks and kudos to many readers for the help with this book. It was challenging to me to start this arc. Many thanks to James Caplan. First reader. Cheerleader. And a guy who constantly has my back. He's going to hate me for calling him a cheerleader. I'll deal with it.

If you thought that Bob the blob thing was smart, well thank Ron and Lisa Frett for giving me the inspiration. I went onto the Facebook group and asked the readers to give me ideas of what they wanted to see in the next arc. See! I listen!

Diane Brenner, Ron Gailey and Tracey Brynes helped to craft the Chief Engineer. Sorry she doesn't have a dragon like you all wanted, but I did give her a ferret. If you're looking for a dragon then hop over to my Orcieran series, Soul Stone Mage. Yes, that's a shameless plug. Come on, my kid goes through shoes like they're packs of chewing gum.

You all had to notice the cars. Before you wonder if I've made besties with a mechanic, the answer is no. When I asked for input from the readers, I also asked for cars they'd like to see included in Hatch's lab. I think you know now that the list of suggestions was overwhelming and I now have to write 45 more books to include them all. Julianna and Eddie will be old and 300 years will have passed before I list the last car suggested by readers. But I will do it!

Thank you to Ron Gailey for suggesting the classic Stutz Bearcat, Roll Royce Silver Shadow and Edsel. Edward Rosenfeld gets the credit for the Buggatti. Micky Cocker gave me the idea for the VW Beetle. Tracey Byrnes had the genius idea to include the 1970 Plymouth Cuda. Kelly O'Donnell was smart to recommend the 57 Corvette. Diane L. Smith when you mentioned the DeLorean, I got giddy. What is Hatch and Knox up to with that car? Also thanks for the idea for the Dodge Charger 440 Magnum. Joe Usakowski, your input on the 76 Cadillac Fleetwood 60 Special Talisman and its spectacular interior is going to make me look smart. And lastly, thank you to James Homet for suggesting the blue 1966 Corvette convertible.

John C. Calvert, you get the final kudo for the idea for Pip's body. You're one clever guy. Michael and I actually discussed the idea a while ago for an AI to control a body. That idea disappeared until you shot this over and I was like, "Yahoo!" Thanks to everyone for all the wonderful suggestions. More to come in books 6 through 49.

Okay, without further ado, I give you the man of the hour. The one you've all been waiting to hear from.

— Sarah

First, thank you for not only reading this story, but reading these Author Notes as well!

Sarah is a sweetie, and to learn that she was able to come from a group of siblings that were so challenging is a bit surprising (because of her sweetness!) It certainly points to people being able to mature to become cool people, no matter what the crap they had to deal with in the beginning.

I didn't suffer this trouble with siblings in my life. For myself, my older brother was pretty cool... Mostly.

I'm the troublemaker, he wasn't. He was the oldest who excelled at school, making the Principle's list and doing all sorts of really amazing scholastic shit that I never lived up to.

Way to make me try harder there, Darryl!

Yes, my character Darryl (or Darrell depending on how I fucked up the spelling) of the Queen's Bitches was named after my older brother. It also explains why the character's name changed in time… I couldn't 'not' spell it the way I knew it to be spelled for 40 years.

So, write that rule down. If you name someone after a sibling, perhaps DON'T change the spelling of their name so that later in the series you correct yourself subconsciously. You will forget the AMAZING idea that 'no one will realize I'm naming this character after my brother' about book 3 or 4…

At least that is what I did.

Later in my life, when I had moved out of the house (18 or 19 at the time) and Darryl and I were sharing an apartment (split plan, he got the better room and paid $10 more a month… That was big money to me in 1986) he did something that I STILL feel like is the pivotal moment in our life together.

I needed two tires and I was making just over minimum wage and going to college. Plus, I was willing to chance a wreck, thinking that it wouldn't happen to me (money problems). Darryl noticed the issues on my car, and he told me that he would pay for ALL four tires to be replaced. Not just cheap tires (which would have been my pick) but good tires at Sam's Wholesale where he had worked, and I was working at that time.

There is no way to express, thirty years later even, how much that act of love means to me even to this day.

I've been able to help Darryl make a few dreams come true in his life since that moment. However, even though the size of the 'payback' is different, I don't know that I will ever feel like I've given him enough back for that example of love to me. I was starving (and didn't know it) to feel wanted and he provided that feeling.

Forever.

So, before I break down in tears while I'm in a room with 200 people, I'll close these Author Notes with a message he will probably *NEVER* read.

And I'm ok with that. The message isn't to him anyway. It's to let you know that I love my older brother, and I'm proud of him.

Ad Aeternitatem,

Michael Anderle

P.S. – This last Thanksgiving, my youngest son Joey Anderle (the author) noticed that his twin brothers car had a spare tire on the rear passenger side, because his brother had messed up his tire.

I never noticed it.

Joey is so tight with his money, that he still has income from his books from over a year ago. However, he went to his brother and told him that he would drive with him to Discount Tire and pay to have that tire replaced because it wasn't safe to be traveling the hours from Texarkana to DFW.

It cost Joey (probably) the same amount of money that my older brother paid 30 years ago.

He (Joey) will also probably never read these author notes.... But in the quiet of Thanksgiving week, 2017, he made his dad very proud, choked up, and wiping tears from his eyes at the type of man he was becoming.

ACKNOWLEDGMENTS

SARAH NOFFKE

Thank you to Michael Anderle for taking my calls and allowing me to play in this universe. It's been a blast since the beginning.

Thank you to Craig Martelle for cheering for me. I've learned so much working with you. This wild ride just keeps going and going.

Thank you to Jen, Tim, Steve, Andrew and Jeff for all the work on the books, covers and championing so much of the publishing.

Thank you to our beta team. I can't believe how fast you all can turn around books. The JIT team sometimes scares me, but usually just with how impressively knowledgeable they are.

Thank you to our amazing readers. I asked myself a question the other day and it had a strange answer. I asked if I would still write if trapped on a desert island and no one would ever read the books. The answer was yes, but the feeling connected to it was different. It wouldn't be as much fun to write if there wasn't awesome readers to share it with. Thank you.

Thank you to my friends and family for all the support and love.

THE GHOST SQUADRON

by Sarah Noffke and Michael Anderle

WANT MORE?

ENTER

THE KURTHERIAN GAMBIT UNIVERSE

A desperate move by a dying alien race transforms the unknown world into an ever-expanding, paranormal, intergalactic force.

The Kurtherian Gambit Universe contains more than 100 titles in series created by Michael Anderle and many talented co-authors. For a complete list of books in this phenomenal marriage of paranormal and science fiction, go to:

http://kurtherianbooks.com/timeline-kurtherian/

ABOUT SARAH NOFFKE

Sarah Noffke, an Amazon Best Seller, writes YA and NA sci-fi fantasy, paranormal and urban fantasy. She is the author of the Lucidites, Reverians, Ren, Vagabond Circus, Olento Research and Soul Stone Mage series. Noffke holds a Masters of Management and teaches college business courses. Most of her students have no idea that she toils away her hours crafting fictional characters. Noffke's books are top rated and best-sellers on Kindle. Currently, she has eighteen novels published. Her books are available in paperback, audio and in Spanish, Portuguese and Italian.

SARAH NOFFKE SOCIAL

Website: http://www.sarahnoffke.com
Facebook: https://www.facebook.com/officialsarahnoffke
Amazon: http://amzn.to/1JGQjRn

a psychic power. Desperate to do whatever it takes to earn her gift, she endures painful daily injections along with commands from her overbearing, loveless father. One of the few bright spots in her life is the return of a friend she had thought dead—but with his return comes the knowledge of a shocking, unforgivable truth. The society Em thought was protecting her has actually been betraying her, but she has no idea how to break away from its authority without hurting everyone she loves.

Rebels, #2

Warriors, #3

VAGABOND CIRCUS SERIES

Suspended, #1

When a stranger joins the cast of Vagabond Circus—a circus that is run by Dream Travelers and features real magic—mysterious events start happening. The once orderly grounds of the circus become riddled with hidden threats. And the ringmaster realizes not only are his circus and its magic at risk, but also his very life.

Vagabond Circus caters to the skeptics. Without skeptics, it would close its doors. This is because Vagabond Circus runs for two reasons and only two reasons: first and foremost to provide the lost and lonely Dream Travelers a place to be illustrious. And secondly, to show the nonbelievers that there's still magic in the world. If they believe, then they care, and if they care, then they don't destroy. They stop the small abuse that day-by-day breaks down humanity's spirit. If Vagabond Circus makes one skeptic believe in magic, then they halt the cycle, just a little bit. They allow a little more love into this world. That's Dr. Dave Raydon's mission. And that's why this ringmaster recruits. That's why he directs. That's why he puts on a show that makes people question their beliefs. He wants the world to believe in magic once again.

Paralyzed, #2

Released, #3

Ren: The Man Behind the Monster, #1

Born with the power to control minds, hypnotize others, and read thoughts, Ren Lewis, is certain of one thing: God made a mistake. No one should be born with so much power. A monster awoke in him the same year he received his gifts. At ten years old. A prepubescent boy with the ability to control others might merely abuse his powers, but Ren allowed it to corrupt him. And since he can have and do anything he wants, Ren should be happy. However, his journey teaches him that harboring so much power doesn't bring happiness, it steals it. Once this realization sets in, Ren makes up his mind to do the one thing that can bring his tortured soul some peace. He must kill the monster.

Note This book is NA and has strong language, violence and sexual references.

Ren: God's Little Monster, #2

Ren: The Monster Inside the Monster, #3

Ren: The Monster's Adventure, #3.5

Ren: The Monster's Death, #4

Twelve men went missing.

Six months later they awake from drug-induced stupors to find themselves locked in a lab.

And on the night of a new moon, eleven of those men, possessed by new—and inhuman—powers, break out of their prison and race through the streets of Los Angeles until they disappear one by one into the night.

Olento Research wants its experiments back. Its CEO, Mika Lenna, will tear every city apart until he has his werewolves imprisoned once again. He didn't undertake a huge risk just to lose his would-be assassins.

However, the Lucidite Institute's main mission is to save the world from injustices. Now, it's Adelaide's job to find these mutated men and protect them and society, and fast. Already around the nation, wolflike men are being spotted. Attacks on innocent women are happening. And then, Adelaide realizes what her next step must be: She has to find the alpha wolf first. Only once she's located him can she stop whoever is behind this experiment to create wild beasts out of human beings.